MEMORIES are FOREVER

(Even as time goes by)

Sarika Giria was born in Kolkata to a loving and affluent family. After finishing her schooling from La Martiniere and graduating from the JD Birla institute, she completed her MBA. Married now for 13 years, her husband Manish Giria owns a highly successful chain of consumer durable stores across South India - GIRIAS. She lives in Bangalore where most of her spare time is dedicated to caring for her two precious children Aman and Sahil. Her interests include traveling, reading and cooking. Writing has always been a passion which she's pursued since her teen years and has now culminated in her first book. You can reach her on sarikagiria@gmail.com @SarikaGiria

MEMORIES are FOREVER

(Even as time goes by)

Sarika Giria

Ocean Paperbacks

A Division of Ocean Books Pvt. Ltd.

ISO 9001:2008 Publishers

Published by
Ocean Paperbacks
A Division of Ocean Books Pvt. Ltd.
4/19 Asaf Ali Road,
New Delhi-110 002 (INDIA)
e-mail: info@oceanbooks.in

ISBN 978-81-8430-271-4
Memories are Forever
by Sarika Giria

Edition
First, 2014

Price
Rs. 150.00 (Rs. One Hundred Fifty only)

Printed at
Bhanu Printers, Delhi

For My Husband
Thank You Manish
For Making This Possible

Author's Note

Every Sunday from the age of six, I would buy books to last me the entire week (this in addition to the ones issued by the school library). Little did I then imagine that one day I would write a book; copies of which would be in those very bookstores I used to frequent as a wide eyed child, waiting to be picked up. Today as I write the author's note, I experience a great sense of pride and fulfillment.

I have to thank my son Aman for helping inspire me with a feasible plot. I was well into my second pregnancy and ready to go into labour at any moment. I informed him about me having to go to the hospital soon to return with a baby sister or brother for him to play with. Instead of being excited he nervously enquired whether I would return or not and what if something bad was to happen to me. I then wrote a letter to him (a sort of goodbye letter just in case something did happen to me). Of course nothing untoward took place and the letter was forgotten. I again chanced upon it just a couple of years ago, when I was dusting my attic and read it to Aman. He had tears in his eyes and hugged me in a tight embrace refusing to let go. At that moment I decided the broad outline of my book.

However, I was far from done. Thinking of the plot was one thing and actually writing it down, a totally different task altogether. For this I have my husband Manish to thank who practically used every trick in the book (and some not in it) to make me get back to writing. Every time I wanted to quit and took up something else, he would motivate, coax, cajole and sometimes even mildly threaten (just kidding) me to carry on with my writing. He even typed for me as my typing skills aren't really anything to write home about (all he asked in lieu was that his name figure prominently in the acknowledgements). Thank you Manish for being instrumental in turning my dreams into reality, without you, this project of mine might have never seen the light of day.

Thank you readers for buying my book and contributing towards a noble cause. Proceeds from the sale of this book will go towards a charitable cause.

Simran who is the main protagonist of my story is a bubbly, cheerful, romantic, dutiful and emotional character. She has a little bit of you, me and all of us. Your regular girl next door, she is a character whom all of us would identify with at some stage or the other. I sincerely hope that my readers will be able to connect with her and enjoy the book.

—Sarika Giria

5th March 2003

My Baby. I can't believe I just wrote that! MY BABY! My child! Wow! It has such a beautiful ring to it. Today, at dawn I discovered that I am pregnant!

I am feeling elated! I am going to become a mother. MOTHERHOOD! You have come into my life. Right now, you are there in me, a tiny bundle of new life growing in my womb.

It is such an amazing feeling. Never have I felt such thrill, such excitement, so much happiness, all together. I was feeling quite jittery before using the home-pregnancy testing kit. Positive or not was the question. If I couldn't conceive now then would it take months more and God forbid, but what if there was a medical complication with either one of us? These negative thoughts amongst quite a few others kept tormenting me, while I impatiently waited for the result to appear. We both shouted out with joy (I am sure it was more an earth shattering shriek), the moment two lines appeared almost as if by magic on the strip. By we, I meant your father (Sameer) and I. Overcome with joy he held me tight and refused to let go. I almost had to push him away, since I couldn't breathe anymore. You see my child, your dad's affection manifests itself in fiercely affectionate hugs, which can sometimes be........... a bit too fierce.

He couldn't contain his joy and said "This calls for a celebration!"

However I was still anxious, "but Sameer, what if the result is *not accurate?* These kits don't guarantee absolute accuracy."

The eternal pessimist in me had yet another negative thought clouding my joy. To erase any lingering doubts from my mind, we decided to get an expert second opinion at the Motherwell Hospital.

It turns out, I needn't have worried so much because pretty soon after, we reaffirmed the joy of your arrival! Yes! I am expecting, and I now sport this huge smile which stretches from one ear to the other. I am still in such a state of euphoric shock; the news is yet to sink in seriously. You can't blame me. This was such a huge event.

Sameer, the ever practical man, immediately reserved an appointment with Dr. Sudha Bhatt, one of Bangalore's leading gynecologists and also a very close friend of my mother-in-law Aruna (actually I should be addressing her as your *Dadi*). Today, I felt such a whirlwind of emotions. There was plenty of excitement, the feeling of incomparable joy tempered with moments of tense anxiety. I am about to embark on the most beautiful journey of my life. I want to share and cherish every moment with you, preserving these memories forever from the fading passage of time; I plan to record all these beautiful emotions in this diary addressed to you. That way, I too can savour these priceless moments with you, years down the road.

6th March

I continue to smile. Well I have reason to grin. Sameer is treating me like a queen.

No *cooking*!

No *cleaning*!

Absolutely no PHYSICAL LABOUR of any sort (that means utensils are out too)!

YIPPEE! I have been told to strictly not to do anything until the doctor gives me the go ahead. Your *dada* and *dadi* (my in-laws) are holidaying in Europe and will be returning in a couple of days. They are as yet unaware about the good news, since we want to surprise them on their arrival. In *dadi*'s absence, Sameer does not want to take any chances, therefore, all I am expected to do is to sit back, relax and be happy. Am I complaining?

Heck no!!!!

I am planning on making hay while the sun shines.

My morning began with your dad serving me breakfast in bed (oooh the sheer redolent luxury of it, sigh). Baked beans on toast, *aloo paranthas*, fruits and a glass of orange juice. Before you jump to conclusions, your dad did not actually cook it. He was never much of a cook. Radha *maasi*, our maid and Raju the cook lent their culinary expertise to the endeavor. Mornings are generally pretty hectic for us and Sameer barely exchanges more than a couple of sentences. Today though, he couldn't stay away from me. Of course you are the one I should thank; else him having a relaxed morning is as rare as the weather forecast being accurate!

I could so get used to being treated like royalty. R-o-y-a-l-t-y. That has a nice ring to it.

The appointment with Dr. Sudha was at 1 o' clock and we left an hour earlier at twelve. The clinic though not round the corner, isn't unmanageably far either. The traffic congestion in our city is not as bad as the other metros, but it was a good thing that we left an hour early. Though normally the time taken to reach the destination would be around 15-20 minutes, today it took thrice as long. The reason? Your dad.

"*Suresh bhaiya, speed 20-25 km ke upar mat le ke jana.*" Can you believe that? The car was crawling forward.

I could swear that on one occasion, a guy even overtook our Mercedes on a BICYCLE! The incessant honking of cars around us was quite embarrassing. Drivers near us were hurling rather unkind, abuses at Suresh *bhaiya*, who, I am sure would have loved to retaliate but had to be on his best behavior at Sameer's insistence.

"*Sab ko ignore kar do. Aap dhere chalo*". We finally managed to reach the clinic, but were greeted with a queue of six expectant mothers ahead of us. Then my better half decided to take matters into his own hands and called up the doctor, imploring her to help us out! This was embarrassing. Within five minutes, I was ushered in ahead of the other patiently waiting ladies, who no doubt would have voiced their indignant protests with the poor receptionist.

Let me introduce you briefly to Dr. Sudha. As you know, she is a very good friend of *dadi's*. She was also her gynecologist and helped bring Sameer into this world as her very first delivery. She has this huge soft corner for him and has been a part in all the important occasions in his life. But it was awkward nonetheless, walking in straight like that (will speak to Sameer about it).

After the routine greetings and enquires about our well-being (especially about my MIL), we showed her our reports.

A large smile bloomed across her face.

Congratulations followed. Then nostalgia set in. She spoke about Sameer being the first child she had helped deliver and now he was going to become a dad. Time sure does fly.

Sameer, ever the concerned husband, kept peppering her with questions and aunty (she was like family and this term of endearment felt apt) kept answering them patiently. I hardly got to ask anything, since Sameer seemed almost prescient in his questions. She checked my vitals. The verdict was in; PERFECT!

Everything was fine. Just a routine ultrasound and a blood test were left before we were good to go. We received a large list of dos and a small list of don'ts. She had a tough time assuring your dad that I was great shape and doing pretty well without requiring any special care with the exception of getting pampered (I would like to admit that I was quite upset as I wanted the status quo to remain).

Your due date is 14 November.

Children's day.

How appropriate. Sameer requested her not to inform *dadi* as he wanted to surprise her with the good news. We left the clinic after what seemed like an interminably long time (your dad had a lot of questions to ask) and on our way out I could feel the angry stares of the six other pregnant women who were there before me. When I got in the car I told Suresh *bhaiya* (Sameer's chauffeur for the past 23 years) to drive back at a more sober speed (won a staring contest with your dad when he was about to open his mouth in protest).

7th March

Opened my eyes early today morning to a lovely sight. My whole room was covered with baby posters! Every nook and cranny of the room had a sweet, cute and smiling baby looking back at me. Some were cute, some chubby and some just downright adorable! I hugged Sameer tightly and admired each image poster with loud exclamations of *oohs* and *aahs*. I did frown a little when I saw baby in a bear's outfit staring at me from the television screen. Did Sameer seriously expect me to spend nine months staring at a bear costumed kid and not watch my (according to him) mindlessly silly stupid *saas-bahu* soap operas? He always complains about them not making any sense and considers them to be a real waste of time. He wants me to watch some good wholesome comedies instead. In my defense however, I would like to state that I also watch a lot of quality sitcoms like Friends, Seinfeld, Everybody loves Raymond amongst many others, I could go on and on (yes your mummy does watch a lot of TV).

Your father is aware of the sizeable time period I spend in the bathroom because there were two posters in there too! That set me wondering as to when he had the time to buy and put them up. He's hardly left my side the last couple of days. I guess he would have purchased it when I was busy picking up some pregnancy books. Speaking of books I did buy quite a few books; nine to be precise. Books on pregnancy, yoga during pregnancy, diet for expectant mothers and even a few on childcare. If Sameer was surprised at the number, he didn't actually show it, except for his raised eyebrows and a startled gasp (quite vocal and in public too) when the cashier informed him about the total sum amounting to Rs. 8800.

More than once he enquired (politely) if I actually intended to read all of them. "*Yoga* Simi? You have never done any deep breathing also. Are you sure you are going to practice it?"

"Just because I have never done it before, does not mean I won't in the future. I have every intention of doing all the asanas that are good for OUR baby" (I guess I should have purchased it in two installments). Anyway, it's not like we can't afford it. Sameer heads our highly successful family business of retail chain stores (which sell garments, accessories, home furnishings and lots more) across the country. So the faux shocked expression was a little too unnecessarily theatrical.

Coming back to the posters the mystery was solved when he said, "Simran I put the posters up during the night when you were sound asleep and snoring blissfully without being aware of its consequences on your husband who happens to be a very light sleeper".

Yes son that did result in an argument. How DARE he say that I SNORE! I so do not. Alright, maybe just a *little* when I am down with a cold, which happens more often than not as Bangalore's weather does not really suit me. The high pollen count in the air is my Achilles heel. The point here though is that I am not going through any nasal congestion right now, so I most certainly couldn't have been snoring. And will wonders never cease? Your dad GAVE IN! He NEVER does that. Now however, he just backed off saying that it was a slip of tongue. I assume that he did not want to upset me.

We both spend the entire afternoon talking about you. "I feel it is going to be a boy", remarked Sameer "No I think it is a girl". I was quick to add. "Then I hope that she takes after you". That was rather sweet of your dad, I am now seeing a totally new side to him. A bit like how it used to be during our courtship days. Let me brief you about our marriage. It is now almost two years since we tied the knot. Ours was an arranged marriage, but love soon followed, we met each other a few times before 'saying yes'. After six months of engagement, we tied the knot.

Those six months were the most beautiful period of my life (until now, obviously your arrival is the most memorable moment since). Sameer would fuss over me and pamper me silly. Long letters, endless calls, lots of gifts and plenty of surprises, but after our wedding, the scenario changed pretty quickly. He immersed himself totally in the daily rigmarole of business and gave up most things that passed for pleasure. I too was trying to adjust to a new city, a new home and a new family. We somehow just did not spend much time with each other. You know what they say "the honeymoon period phase ends with the honeymoon". We fought a lot, had our fair share of arguments and would get into fights over the silliest of reasons (usually started by me). I assume it was because we both got married young. I was 21 and Sameer was not yet 23. But there was always a bond of love tying us to each other. We were two connected souls, a smile on one's face would bring a wider one on the other's. The pain of one would upset the other. We would be happiest in each other's company. Today our love has been further strengthened by your presence.

Seriously, I have never seen Sameer take a break from work (until and unless he is very ill and then it is definitely better to have him at work than at home as he gets very cranky), or spend the whole day doing nothing but being by my side (except on vacations) and fuss over my meals (he feels that I should cut down on my eating; well I've put on a couple of kgs and a few inches in the past year, but hey, I am still a size medium). Every now and then he just says 'thank you'. Honestly, he hasn't stopped thanking me from the time the kit showed those two amazing lines. Well to be fair to him, he too deserves equal credit as he's just as responsible for breathing life into you as I am. But let's not get into the nitty gritties. Rather let me make the most of this moment. So I just reply with an affectionate "you're welcome, love".

8th March

Your *dada-dadi* arrived at two, yesterday night (technically it should be two, this morning). *Dadi* was really tired and just wanted to retire to her room, but they were totally excited (completely anticipated) when we showed them the room decorated with baby pictures! We had done up the room and greeted them with a baby message poster which read "Congratulations *Dada* and *Dadi*-to-be" on their mirror (using *dadi*'s brand new CD lipstick – I hope she forgives me for it). Balloons and streamers (which kept fluttering all night long and did not let them get their much needed sleep; but hey with news of such magnitude their excitement would not have allowed them to get much of it anyways) embellished their room, was my idea and a small doll placed on the pillow (Sameer's brilliant brainwave) completed the ambient décor.

Congratulatory hugs followed along with a volley of questions. "When is the due date?", "How are you doing?", "Did you meet

Sudha?", "Have you been eating properly?" We patiently answered all their queries. I was enjoying my moment of glory when suddenly the focus shifted on Sameer. "Oh, I cannot believe Sameer is now going to become a dad" exclaimed *dada*. Well what is there not to believe? How could they ever doubt it? "Ooooh, soon we will have a tiny Sameer in our arms" said *dadi*.

Now wait a minute – I was supposed to be the center of attention here!!! Hello??? I was pregnant, not their darling Sameer, and what was this all about a tiny Sameer? Why not a tiny Simran? This was not fair. I mean generally your grandparents are really wonderful people and excellent as in-laws, I have always been treated like a daughter (as you know your father is an only child and *dada* had always yearned for a daughter) and mollycoddled by his parents. But somehow I was feeling the pinch of blood being thicker than water just then. The hormonal swings associated with pregnancy had probably been set in motion.

Ok, maybe I was being a little too hasty in thinking so, but it was just natural to expect more attention than Sameer. After all, he wasn't going to be the one carrying you around for the next 9 months, looking like a kangaroo was he? He sensed my emotions and very gracefully and tactfully shifted focus back to me, by thanking me very vocally (especially for *Dadi*'s benefit) "Thank you Simran for bringing this joy in our lives. We all owe our happiness to you."

And once again I was the cynosure of all eyes!

Today, in the, morning your *Nana-Nani* in Kolkata were informed about the good news (we did not want to play favourites and felt that both set of grandparents needed to be told about it together). My eardrum is still reverberating from your *maasi*'s shriek. Simar screeched through the phone and I am pretty sure you heard that too. Your uncle Ravi, who is a year older than me, was much more restrained, but sounded equally happy. *Nana*, *Nani* (to avoid confusing you I am going to refer to Sameer's parents as *dada-dadi* and mine as *nana-nani*) spoke at length and were thrilled at the prospect of a small baby Simran (now I am not selfish, but I did not mind that it was baby Simran and not baby Sameer that was mentioned) gracing their lives soon.

Well this was my moment of glory and your father had better play second fiddle. After all, don't we belong to a land that venerates the notion of a loving Indian mother (all thanks to you darling for allowing me to be one)?

9th March

Feeling sick…the first waves of nausea hit this morning and I promise this has got nothing to do with *dadi* coming back and telling me about the benefits of working throughout pregnancy to ensure a smooth and easy delivery (now is easy delivery not an oxymoron?).

Dadi asked me to supervise the breakfast preparations. She feels that it is very important for us to be fully involved with the cooking aspect, despite having quite a few hands to help us, one of whom is even a great cook. Friends are always amazed that we employ so many helpers, but they are a necessity and not a luxury while managing such a large house and satisfying the expectations of a very finicky MIL. The moment I walked into the kitchen to make *sambhar* (*Idly-sambhar* is our Sunday morning staple), I felt a terrible urge to throw up. The smell of the spices sizzling in the hot oil made my stomach churn. This baffled me since I've never felt anything like this in the past. Then it struck me. Since *dadi* had been travelling to Europe the past few weeks, I had rather conveniently handed over all the responsibilities of the kitchen to Raju and Radha *maasi* and decided to take it easy. To be honest, I have never really enjoyed cooking, though I don't mind it once in a while (more like once in a blue moon). However when you marry into a *Jain* household like ours, you had better take to cooking as a fish takes to water.

All your MIL expects you to do, is cook; not once, but thrice a day, and not just your everyday regular *roti-sabzi*, you also need to be able to whip up fancy five star fare whenever a guest drops in (which is every now and then). Your *dadi* would then take great pride in telling everyone "Oh, please sample this, my *Bahu* has made it. You must have a bit of this, it is her special dish". I was once stupid (silly me) enough to ask "Is there nothing more to do other than cooking?" –and pat came the reply – sewing, stitching, embroidery and painting. I was never the artistic types and this was my definitive foot in the mouth moment. Honestly speaking, I was never a big fan of cooking, treating it as a tedious chore and had gladly handed over the responsibility to my very trusted helpers in *dadi*'s absence.

But at that moment right then, please do believe me when I say that I was not faking it and genuinely felt claustrophobic as if the vapour from the hot oil seemed like it was some sort of noxious fume out there to get me. I felt bile rising within me. Within seconds the chocolate milkshake which I had consumed some time back, found its way to the wash basin, much to the dismay of everyone around me. I was immediately asked to make myself scarce from the kitchen; I didn't need to be told this twice, I was out in a jiffy.

Reading seemed like a good alternative. Nothing broadens your horizons and gives wings to your thoughts the way reading does. I love to read and do so with great zest. Have always felt very possessive about my books and that is why I prefer to buy them, rather than borrow them from a leading library. Your dad keeps joking that I squander half his wealth buying books.

"Sameer I gain knowledge by reading. It improves your

perspective and helps you see the world in a different light." I told him. "How much have you learned by reading more than a thousand *Mills & Boons* and countless *Archies*?" he retorted.

Not having a very strong riposte, I sheepishly ignore his jibe. This always happens to me. All the brilliant retorts and repartees surface a couple of hours too late. Sigh. Hindsight.

Spent the remainder of the afternoon catching up on the reruns of my favourite soaps operas. *Tulsi* from *Ekta Kapoor's "Kyunki Saas Bhi Kabhi Bahu Thi*" was trying to save her family from some crisis when I started craving for a cookie and cream flavored ice-cream. I messaged Sameer; calling him up at this time is never a good idea since he is generally in some meeting. "Your wish is my command", was his endearing reply. Within half an hour, while yet another of *Ekta Kapoor's* brilliantly perfect *bahu* (now why does the daughter-in-law need to live up to such high standards is beyond me) tries to set right her scheming MIL, the driver delivered the ice-cream. I open the box to find two half liter tubs of bliss! My favorite flavor packed in dry ice to prevent it from melting. He really did think of everything, but there was no way that I could polish of this huge quantity desire notwithstanding.

Two hours of channel surfing and two tubs of ice-cream later, I had gently dozed off to sleep.

11th March

Could not write to you yesterday, but it was pretty much the same as the day before. Threw up yet again after trying to make mushrooms in garlic sauce and it was *unani*mously decided that I was not to venture into the kitchen for at least a few weeks. Who was I to argue with the diktats of the family elders?

I was a little nervous today since it was my first ultrasound scan. Sameer and I had gone to a larger, more well-known hospital. We had to wait (there was no Sudha aunty this time around to speed up the process) for more than an hour before it was our turn. A large machine with a display screen was placed near my bed. The nurse then applied a really thick, sticky, gooey gel (which later refused to yield to the relentless application of any number of tissue papers) after which the technician commenced the ultrasound.

Within seconds, the image of my uterus was being displayed on the screen. I looked out for you, but could see nothing. I panicked and squeezed Sameer's hand, while he stood next to me totally glued to the screen. "Where's my baby doctor?" "This tiny circle that you see – that's the foetus".

It sounded weird to hear the doctor address you so, but what agitated me was that I was unable to figure out which circle she was referring to. Boy, was I disappointed!! I had imagined that I would see a small baby and instead had to make do and be excited about some circle (which I was anyway unable to make out).

"That's the bubble is it not?" said a delighted Sameer and the doctor nodded in acknowledgement. Now that got me even more irritated. Even your dad could see it. I then gave up. The doctor in the meantime took the measurement of the uterus, the ovaries and the cervix.

"Everything is absolutely fine", she assured us.

18th March

Have been feeling very weak and dizzy lately especially in the mornings. Feel very drained out in the first half of the day. It feels like a blanket of lethargy has been wrapped around me. Don't feel like eating, talking or doing anything.

The not eating aspect is currently everybody's major concern.

With great difficulty, I manage to force myself to have a few spoonfuls of all the dishes that *dadi* goes about preparing for me. But I end up puking even that in a matter of minutes. All this throwing up has now left me with a permanently aching stomach. I don't understand this sudden repulsion to food. I am (no, was) a big time foodie. Live to eat and love to eat was the mantra I had been following all my life. Sameer often used to joke that me and food were opposite poles and hence always attracted each other. But now, he too was worried as I had lost some more weight. *Dadi* re-assured him that this was a very normal situation, especially in the first trimester, but that didn't stop him from worrying. He keeps getting takeaways (knowing how much I used to relish them before) and is continuously monitoring my meals. This is getting on to me.

I am fed up of everybody asking me to eat.

BACK OFF EVERYONE

Leave me alone.

26th March

This has been a *REALLY baaaad* fortnight. Continued to lose weight and have started looking very pale. I met Sudha aunty yesterday for a routine checkup along with Sameer and *dadi*. I felt so weak that just getting there seemed to be an ordeal. This time I felt no guilt at jumping the line. *Dadi* and Sudha aunty greeted each other like two long lost friends.

After they were finally done with their pleasantries (which took quite a while and seemed like an eternity especially since I felt I would pass out any moment) they shifted their attention to me. My vitals seemed well in order, which was confirmed by Sudha aunty.

"There is nothing to get alarmed about Aruna (*dadi*), this

weight loss is common in the first trimester, but Simran it is important that you follow a healthy diet".

She then briefed me about the importance of a well-balanced diet and how essential it was for the growth of the baby. God please help me! No! I could not go through yet another lecture. I am a well-educated woman who is also armed with the combined knowledge of almost a dozen pregnancy books (all I had done the past few weeks was read – and I am well aware that food is an essential ingredient for my baby's and my well-being). But for God's sake, there are sometimes when you just don't feel like eating or are just unable to eat. It is not that I am willfully depriving myself of food or that I enjoy feeling weak all the time. It is just that I can't eat.

In the midst of all this, your dad wasn't helping either. "Aunty I am really worried about her. Simran used to love food. In fact, she was one of those gourmand types who live to eat rather than eat to live. Please try to make her understand the need for a proper diet".

I had to do all I could, to keep myself from kicking him hard in front of his mom and my doctor.

7th April

The third month of the pregnancy has begun today. The nausea has decreased (thank goodness for it) and is now confined to only morning sickness. Have started having frequent small meals but I am still unable to keep it in. Constant bouts of vomiting have left me lighter still (oh they should be advertising this as effective weight loss therapy- if you can withstand the puking) by another kg.

We hadn't yet informed relatives and friends about you as it is generally assumed that sharing of the good news should be done on the onset of the fourth month (so as not to jinx it). However anyone who dropped in to visit, took one look at me and immediately enquired if there was "good news in the offing".

It seems like it has been ages now since I last have stepped out of the house. Exhaustion was the reason for this self-imposed house arrest. Don't even have the energy to catch up on movies, go out and meet friends or even indulge in some much needed shopping (I cannot even begin to tell you how much I miss it; and I am sure even the malls would have noticed my absence). Books and the television are my two constant companions. Either I am reading or channel surfing. I also played a lot of board games with Sameer which I always ended up winning (I suspect that has a lot to do with me getting upset at having lost a game previously and spend the rest of the evening sulking. After which, I am yet to lose a game to your dad).

15th April

Nausea seems to be reducing and my appetite seems to have improved (much to Sameer's relief). I have also started heading out again. Caught up with my friends for lunch today at Little Italy. Spend the entire afternoon chatting with Priyanka, Sneha, Shabnam, Raina and Julie. Had a real good time.

We spoke about the latest *Salmaan Khan* release *Tere Naam* a must watch movie, as everyone was raving about it with the exception of Julie who is a diehard *Shahrukh Khan* fan (the other Khans just don't cut it for her). Caught on what the grapevine had to say about the current sales happening at the malls (now I was never the one to give up on a good sale), indulged in a little bit of gossip (the harmless type and with no malice whatsoever) and followed it up with the usual complaints about 'MILs' (I solemnly promise that I was not a part of this, as your *dadi* is a sweetheart and deserved no such treatment. She is a real gem if you can ignore her obsession with cleanliness).

"So Simran what is the secret of your recently acquired size zero figure?" enquired the grey-green eyed Sneha who always liked to flaunt her perfectly slim figure (did I detect a tinge of jealousy in her voice?).

OH MY GOD!

No one had yet figured out that I was pregnant. Not that it was supposed to be that obvious. This was just my third month and my belly was still looking pretty toned (a little soft maybe, but definitely toned). I was to be the first in the group to savour motherhood. (Julie wasn't even married yet). What was I supposed to do? Couldn't let the cat out of the bag with news right now, could I?– was too confused as to whether should I share the news of my pregnancy or wait for the stipulated period of three months to be over.

"Yeah Simi, are you following some new diet or have you finally hit the gym after promising to do so to melt away all those five course meals that we have had together? Please pass on your secret na, even I need to trim a few kilos off" asked Raina while chewing on a slice of pizza with extra cheese, washing it down with a glass of soda. I wanted to show her a mirror and tell her that she didn't just need to "trim a few pounds" but a whole lot more. And additionally, if she continued to eat the way she did then very soon she would be requiring 'tent sized XXL' clothing.

"But Simi all the weight loss has drained your face of colour. You are looking very pale", observed Shabnam.

How I longed to tell them that my new diet was a few nibbles of this and a bite of that which was followed by a mandatory puking session which undid all my eating. I was itching to tell them the reason and debated with myself (all this with a straight face). Finally, calmed myself down and reached the decision that I would wait till we met again next month (we catch up once every month). I do admit that it was so difficult for me not to share this wonderful news. Deep within me a voice kept telling me to announce it loud and clear – share it with one and all. After all, this was a beautiful phase of my life which would bring joy to my near and dear ones. Why should I deny them this happiness? Ok I am just talking crap. Basically, it is very difficult for me to keep a secret.

So to avoid further cognitive dissonance, I devoted all my energy in consuming the heavenly wood burnt thin crust pizza with a delicious overdose of cheese. "Let's just not talk about weight and sizes. Instead enjoy our delicious lunch", I said while relishing a sizeable portion of penne in pesto sauce.

It was a great afternoon and I enjoyed it thoroughly, laughing and eating with much gusto (to the delight of Sameer who was surprised that I had polished off three slices of pizza, pasta, a medium portion of risotto and before I forget, an utterly delectable tiramisu). The icing on the cake was that for a change I did not throw up. Nothing uplifts your mood like enjoying a good time with your friends. And am I glad that we formed this girlie group of eight (of those that weren't there, Pinky was travelling to South Africa and Rachna was down with viral fever so could not make it today).

Shabnam and I had known each other from the precocious age of ten. We had done our schooling together in Kolkata. Sneha and Rachna were the wives of Sameer's friends. Pinky and Raina were Rachana's cousins, Julie and Priyanka were Sneha's family friends. It is now more than a year since we have known each other. We like to believe that we are friends in need and would gladly lend one another a shoulder to cry on (not that anybody has yet needed one).

Felt my spirits buoyed and I was in a far more cheerful mood than earlier. Hunger pangs were making themselves felt again and I was once more craving for a pizza. Maybe I might just order one from Pizza Hut.

23rd April

Totally hooked on to pizzas. Gorging on them everyday. This was unfortunately not going down well with *dadi*. She was really glad initially, that I had finally started eating something without throwing up (the morning sickness still pursues me now and again; sometimes within a matter of minutes the breakfast finds its way out of me forcefully) but as she saw it develop into a habit and a daily one at that she tried to talk me out of cramming in the 'fast food junk'.

"Mummy let her eat. Something is better than nothing. Besides there are plenty of vegetables on the pizza", said Sameer my knight in shining armour, always ready to rescue me in any 'tight' situation. *Dadi* reluctantly nodded her head in agreement.

Somehow MILs listen and understand better when their sons put forward a proposition as opposed to the poor daughters-in-law. For instance, this one time when I kept dropping subtle hints about denims and dresses being acceptable vestments nowadays (we hail from a traditional Jain family where the women usually wear sarees and salwar suits), she had a shocked look on her face. "Simran please, what will our society say? They will keep talking for months behind our backs, and I am not sure this would be acceptable to your father".

Now this statement was totally wrong. She need not have used poor *dada* as an excuse to express her personal opinion. *Dada* is the most chilled out person I know. He has never been bothered by what people say. Also, I am the apple of his eye and he likes to pamper me silly. He always supports me in every argument that I have with Sameer (even if I am in the wrong!).

"Mom there is a certain dress code in pubs and lounges. Either she dresses accordingly or we don't go". Sameer puts his point forth in an absolute no nonsense manner. Result – Got the green signal!

24th April

Why? Why? Why? Just why is she coming? Pushpa *bhua* (*dada's* elder sister and a strict disciplinarian) is coming over for a couple of weeks (to make my life miserable). Yes, it's her brother's house and she is entitled to visit and no, she is not exactly Attila the Hun. It's just that her large list of "dos and absolutely don'ts" means that she can aspire to the title. She looks like a character straight out of the movies. In her presence, we are all changed personalities.

I am especially prone to total metamorphosis. She still does not know about my pregnancy (in her own words – stay mum about becoming a mum until three months are over) and when she does, boy will my lifestyle change drastically. I already shudder at the thought of her replacing all my Bollywood numbers (which I currently listen to most of the time) with religious and devotional hymns (I too find peace and tranquility in the Navkar Mahamantra but not on a 24/7 basis). Out go the jeans and in come the salwar suits; *dadi* will have to perpetually be in sarees. There are however, (as unusual as it sounds) a couple of people who look forward to her visits. Radha *maasi* and Raju, since they get plenty of rest as mummy and me have to do all the cooking. "The ladies must handle the affairs of the kitchen irrespective of how many domestic helpers one has" is one of her enduring refrains. I could actually go on and on about her and end up writing a book! She would honestly make a very interesting character (albeit only in a book). I had once cheekily asked *dada* if she really was his own sister, as their similarity ended with their noses and brown eyes (other than that, they were poles apart).

I guess I shouldn't behave like this. I know it is pretty narrow-minded of me to think of her in this manner. If Ravi was to get married tomorrow, I wouldn't like his wife to blanch at my arrival in Kolkata (not that I will ever give her reason to do so). I would be a wonderful sister-in- law and we would bond like soul sisters. She would be able to entrust me with all her secrets. Our days together would be spent in shopping, chatting and hanging out at the best restaurants. We would be each other's BFFs. When it would be time to depart and head back home after my annual visit, there would be tears of sadness in her eyes. Now wait a minute! What am I thinking about? Ravi has not yet got married and I am already daydreaming about my relationship with his wife. I guess I got carried away with my thoughts. No wonder they say that the mind can travel faster than anything else. If Sameer ever caught hold of my diary then he would laugh his head off and tease me no end (he as yet, does not know about it).

Coming back to our original subject 'Pushpa *bhua*', we are now on high alert. I have started counting down the days before she arrived and changed the blissfully happy status quo we're currently enjoying.

26th April

Had a superb day! Fantastic! Sameer took the entire day off from work. First we went out for breakfast at 'Chalukya' one of the most popular south indian restaurants in the city. Two *idlis* and a *vada* later we headed out to shop. He asked me to pick up maternity clothes for the coming months in the hope that I would start putting on weight soon and have a nice big tummy to show for it. Now this was a good reason to shop (not that I needed an excuse ever to go shopping). In fact, shopping is a proven solution to many of my problems. Had a bad day? Go shopping! Too much stress? Shopping is the answer. Want to celebrate an occasion? What better way than to shop? A change in clothing size (hopefully for the better) and shopping becomes an absolute necessity.

Darn it! Who am I kidding? I am almost a shopaholic (use the term almost because I won't go through a nervous breakdown if I don't pick stuff which I won't need or will never use) and can never say no to any kind of bargain or sale. But in my defense I would very pointedly like to ask which girl (woman actually) doesn't like to shop? Almost everyone in my gender would be able to write a book on 1001 reasons to go shopping and before it's even printed, a sequel would already be in the works.

Sameer on the other hand is not too particularly fond of it. He likes to pick up his stuff once every four months. He knows exactly what he wants, heads to that particular counter, picks up what he likes to fit with his physique, (which is perpetually medium, despite all the food that he tucks into, talk about luck). I, though, have to keep a constant watch on my calorie intake and exercise regularly to not gain weight, while he has to just sit back and let his metabolism do all the work. Anyway, I don't think your dad knows how to shop. I always have to pick something up to match his slim physique, fair complexion and brown eyes (they are to die for!). Also, what fun is shopping if you don't try on different styles, multiple colours, and various sizes and finally end up buying what you never thought you would in the first place? Also since you never picked up what you had originally wanted to purchase, you have a very legitimate excuse to go and indulge yourself yet again.

I was in a pretty jovial mood till I stepped in this childcare boutique. Around me there were many pregnant women with a very prominent bulge. There were tiny socks and shoes. Kids clothes so small that they would be considered too tiny even for a doll. Around me were new-born babies and tiny tots in prams looking absolutely adorable! These sights bought forth a surge of emotions within me. Felt a flutter in my stomach, a tightening in my chest and moistness in my eyes. A child is a gift from God. There is no joy greater than that of motherhood. My bundle of happiness was within me growing up safe and sound. Guess I was just overwhelmed at the thought of both of us together. I was so grateful to God for letting me experience this great joy of motherhood. Didn't realize that I had started to cry then, but Sameer did. And despite my repeated assurances that all was fine, he did not seem convinced and kept looking puzzled and confused, so I finally gave up trying to convince him. Men have never been able to understand women and probably never will.

After a quiet lunch (didn't feel like talking too much) we went on to watch *Veer Zaara* (no nausea or fatigue for a change) in the newly opened plush gold class section of the forum mall. Julie had raved about the cinematic experience in this particular theatre and for a change she was right. It was totally comfort viewing. For starters they have a lounge with decadent sofas where you were served lemonade with chips and peanuts while you flipped over their coffee table books. Then you are guided to your seats which are 180 degrees recliner sofas. For your comfort a pillow and blanket are provided. To top it all there is a buzzer on the side of the recliners which beckon an attendant who takes down your order and soon a selected assortment of gourmet dishes are placed for your personal consumption on your own private table. WOW! An absolutely mind-blowing experience. Also the movie was nice too.

We ended our perfect day with a long drive and a couple of scoops of my favorite ice cream. I loved every minute of the day today. In fact, I thought that it was a perfect day. Then just to remind me how perfection does not last forever, my wonderful day had to end on a sour note. Pushpa *bhua* had called up to give the flight details of her arrival. So I would like to conclude by saying that it was an "almost" perfect day.

27th April

Chatted, chatted and then chatted some more; spoke so much that at the end of the day Sameer quipped, "Simi just because God has given you a tongue doesn't mean you have to use it all the time".

So what did we speak about? At the breakfast table we spoke about the BIG issue – your name. We had all been thinking of a few options but weren't yet convinced. I had liked *Shania* if you were to be a girl and *Shreyanz* if you were to be a boy. Whereas Sameer wanted *Samarath* and *Sameera.* "Come on Simi it is naturally logical for Sameer's daughter to be *Sameera.* It has such a nice ring to it".

"I am so sorry Mr. Sameer Jain but I fail to understand how this happens to be a logically drawn conclusion". "Love I am the father, I too have a right to name my child". "More than that of a mother? No. I don't think so. Just try falling pregnant. Going through morning sickness, nausea, disfigurements, a belly resembling that of a giant panda and let me not even get started on the subject of labour. Then comeback and talk to me about rights". The anger was now evident in my voice.

"Yes of course the glorified mother. Do you have any idea of what we men ever go through? Dealing with your mood swings which if including pre-menstrual syndrome, menstrual syndrome and post-menstrual syndrome last about 25 days a month. You ask me if you are looking fat in a dress. If I reply with a yes, it means I don't love you and if I say no, then I am lying. You want me to achieve success but I am supposed to give you plenty of time every day simultaneously. When I take you out shopping you expect me to pick up things which you like without letting me know what you want, like I am some sort of a mind reader!

You want to discuss what we don't like about each other so we can change for the other's benefit, but the minute I open my mouth, tears start rolling down your cheeks. You never fight fair. I know you are pregnant but have you noticed me trying to take care of all your needs? Taking time out from work whenever you wish so, holding your head when you throw up, and later massaging your shoulder and neck to make you feel better. Worrying myself sick about what you eat, trying to do everything possible so that you always stay happy. All the while hearing you crib and complain incessantly. Just a few days back you were upset that I came home 15 minutes later than promised, but yesterday you kept me waiting for 45 minutes while you were getting ready. But I was obviously supposed to understand.... OUCH!

I aimed my slipper at him and found my aim to be true when it found its mark. I thought he was going to get angry, but he only had this baffled look and told me while nursing his elbow, "Thank God you picked up the rubber slipper and not the glass vase. That would have hurt a lot more". We both laughed and called a truce by hugging.

I sent him a lot of texts and lovey-dovey messages through the day (on occasions up to 10 a minute) and he sweetly sent a reply to almost all of them. Later in the night I apologized for hitting him with a slipper. "It's ok sweetheart. You can use anything light and soft and do try to always avoid hard objects. I did observe that your aim has improved, that is if you were not targeting my head."

"Sameer I realized how much you actually do for me. Always giving in to all my tantrums and whims. Fulfilling my every wish. Losing all the games we play just so that I can smile. Pampering me no end". He started to smile, so I quickly added "I want this treatment to last not just for my pregnancy but long after that. You can stop looking so shocked. I am upgrading you to a 'dad' so I rightfully deserve to be treated like a queen all my life".

The look on his mum face was priceless!

30th April

Pushpa *bhua* has arrived! As she entered, out walked my peace of mind. To be fair, also add my MIL's sanity. Just why is she's like this and how on earth does her husband manage to put up with her? Nobody knows. Forget about her husband, it is her two poor DILs who have all my sympathies. I am going to rant a bit more here, bear with me sweetie. Just who does she think she is and what right does she have to tell us how to live our lives? How on earth is she so sure about her decisions for us being better than our own?

What am I doing? I am not supposed to be getting upset. Sorry sweetheart, but she can be a real pain in the neck. Let me narrate the events of the day lest you start accusing me of exaggeration (like your dad always does). She arrived by the morning flight (and just this once the airline had to land before time). She was dressed in a georgette saree and no nonsense flat slippers. Her waist length hair was tied neatly into a bun and believe me when I tell you, not a strand was out of place! Though she is about my height, she appears shorter because of her stocky build. Her sharp features look a little out of place on her round face.

It started with "Why are you not carrying a duppatta, Simran beta?" in response to me touching her feet for her blessings. "Oops! Forgot it in the kitchen *bhua*". "Glad to hear that you have started entering the kitchen once in a while". Was there truly any need for her to taunt me thus? In reply to her sarcastic comment, a thousand witty retorts were flitting through my mind but they unfortunately were not vocalized. So all I did was smile back (with pressed lips), but if looks could kill then it would have been a different story all together.

To break the tension which had started to seep in, *dadi* gently broke the news of my pregnancy. And lo behold! The eighth wonder of the world materialised in front of me. She actually smiled, and a quite a wide one at that. A gentle hug and a few words of congratulations (she does not believe in over-doing anything) followed by a never-ending list of instructions. I wonder why we bother going to Dr Sudha when we have our very own Pushpa *bhua* who probably feels she is better qualified than certified doctors. After an hour (I am sure the watch had it wrong for it definitely felt like an eternity hearing her monologue), I politely informed her that I was leaving so that I could lie down for a while. That was all the opening she needed before beginning with:

"In our times we would have to do everything ... and we continued working till our due date... these girls today have it so easy. They just imagine that they are tired. It is the MILs who are to be blamed. They have grown too soft…now my MIL had ensured that I work normally till child birth and that benefitted both me and my children". Needless to say I had to forego my rest.

After serving her lunch and escorting her to her room, I ran back to mine and locked it so that she didn't intrude on me. *Hritik Roshan* was doing gravity defying moves to the tune of *Ay mere dil tu gaaye ja* from *Kaho Na Pyaar Hai* when *bhua* knocked (it was not even an hour). Before opening the door I switch off the TV and hastened to straighten my room. Everything that seemed out of place was quickly dumped into Sameer's cupboard. It has a lot more space than mine. She walked in briskly before I could slip out. After inspecting my room with her darting eyes, she proceeded to give me yet another lecture (yes, you guessed it right) on the benefits of hearing chants and mantra's and its effects on the unborn child. She must have heard me playing Bollywood numbers (though I can vouch for the volume being inaudible). She then played the *Navkaar Mahamantra* (*dadi* has a whole selection of these CDs). If I was not seething with anger at that moment, I would have probably admitted to being calmed by the soothing effect of the chant.

The next salvo was to be launched on my eating habits (apparently unhealthy according to her). Why did *dadi* have to tell her about my pizza binging? Betrayed by my own MIL. With the passage of time, I had learnt about all the harmful effects about 'outside food' and how *maida* 'the white poison' killed the body slowly but surely. "Simran is this the kind of nutrition you want to pass on to your child? Think about your child, a baby who has no say in your food choices but who alone has to suffer its poisonous effects".

Talk about exaggeration! Now only if *dada* or Sameer were here. Why were they never around when I needed them the most?

First my work habits, then my music, next my diet and then she started to drone about T.V viewing habits. So what if I watch endless pot boilers or mindless serials (as she calls them)!

How does it matter if I derive nothing knowledgeable from them? What is her Goddamn problem? Why can't she mind her own business? She cannot tell me what to watch and what not to. Just waiting for the day to end. Come to think of it, today was just the first of a long fortnight. Sameer please come to my rescue.

5th May

Ran away from home! Not in the actual sense. Just escaped to Dr. Sudha's clinic for a check-up. I was actually supposed to go the day after (after completing my second ultrasound) but I couldn't take any more of Pushpa *bhua* and just had to have a break. To kill time I did not allow Sameer to jump the line.

"Simi there are 7 ladies ahead of us. It will take at least an hour. Please let me talk to Sudha aunty", pleaded Sameer. "Don't you even think about it. I am in no hurry. The longer it takes, the better it is. Just because she is your aunty you cannot keep barging in, out of turn, every time. All the other husbands are patiently waiting (which was a blatant lie as most of the guys were preoccupied with their phones or laptops and kept stealing glances at their watches every two minutes while impatiently tapping their feet). Now please let me read for a while". Before he could respond, I studiously buried my nose in an *Archie* comic. I am a big fan of comics and even now pick up every new comic available. Today I was armed with eight double digests and could bide my time easily. That was when *nani* called up. She enquired about my well-being and then it struck me. Why don't I escape to Kolkata? Away from Pushpa *bhua*, amidst heavenly food, and lots of lazing around? Good idea!

Must talk to Sameer about it. He was of course talking on the phone (an entire hour! And women get blamed for talking too long!). Not that I missed chatting, I was busy reading remember?

Finally it was our turn. Weight – a slight increase (yippee! Finally gaining some), BP – perfectly normal (now this was surprising as I had anticipated it to be on the higher side thanks to Pushpa *bhua*). Sudha aunty looked pleased when she said "Good progress Simran, you have started gaining weight, BP is normal and you are looking much better too. Just email me your ultrasound reports. Everything looks fine, so enjoy your pregnancy".

"Is it ok for me to take a flight to Kolkata now?" no sooner had I asked this question then Sameer almost jumped out his seat. There was actually no need for him to react like that. Alright, I did not forewarn him, but hey, I Just wanted to plan a trip to my mom's place (every girl's right after marriage).

Dr Sudha looked puzzled, exchanged glances with Sameer before replying very cautiously. "We will wait for the ultrasound reports and then take a call".

The entire distance to Windsor Manor (I had insisted on having lunch there, just love their north Indian fare there and also to stay away for some more time from home) I tried to convince him that this was the best time for me to take off to Kolkata for my annual holiday.

"Let us first get the ultrasound done and then discuss this please" was his rather terse reply. After dropping Sameer to the office I went shopping to soothe my frayed nerves. Spent time trying out various stilettos before finally settling for 3 pairs of flat shoes and slippers. I needed to look out for good flat sandals as I had now been told to bid goodbye to all my pencil heels and stilettos (needed them to stand up to your tall father who appears even taller than his 6 feet height because of his lanky built). I then indulged myself in picking up quite a few *Asterix* comics (which I intended to read once *bhua* leaves). She would have had a fit if she saw me laughing over the antics of the short, irrepressible *Gaul* warrior who along with his pig-tailed, lumbering companion *Obelix* never failed to amuse me. With the nausea diminishing along with the morning sickness, I wasn't throwing up too often. This had elevated my energy levels and moving around was no longer tiring. I now enjoyed my outings (especially with *bhua* waiting for me at home). I killed as much time as possible before heading home.

The evening was spent in preparing *biryani* along with different vegetables and *rotis*, not to mention plenty of sweets. We *Marwari's* are obsessed with cooking. Our day starts and ends with it. Our entire life can pass by in a clouded haze of aromatic odours from the kitchen and we might not even happen to realize it. Almost every other community will settle for one main dish served with rice or *chappatis*. But not us. Oh no siree! We need two or three vegetables (one of which has to be a rich gravy and loaded with calories), different kinds of *rotis* and a mandatory rice preparation. Curds, salads and dessert have to be served too and this is just the daily menu! No wonder most of us suffer from cholesterol or diabetes. And when a guest arrives, the menu grows in complexity if anything along with the hours spent in the kitchen. This is what our womenfolk have been doing for generations and we are expected to follow suit. Pushpa *Bhua* loved the biryani I made and helped herself to three servings while complimenting me, "You cook very well Simran, try spending more time in the kitchen". Compliment or sarcasm-you try to figure it out.

7th May

Completed 3 months of my pregnancy. So happy this phase is over. Everyone around is always asking you to be extra cautious during this period. Now I can relax (not that I wasn't earlier).

I went for a scan today. Sameer (will never miss a scan, though he had been complaining of the hours that he had to take off from work just so that he can accompany me on my 'pleasure trips') and *dadi* (who wanted to see a moving image of you) came along. After the mandatory waiting for almost an hour (why do they bother giving appointments if they don't stick to their timings) my turn came up. I asked a few questions to the resident doctor (Dr Renu) regarding your vitals and anxiously waited for your image to pop up on screen. Then I saw you. A tiny head on a tiny body. Your head swayed gently from side to side. Both *dadi* and Sameer were very excited and their joy was palpable, while I lay there overcome with emotion. I then heard your heartbeat. A whooping 180 (sounded more like a large horse galloping). Felt connected to you and did not want the moment to end. You had finally grown from an indistinct blot which I couldn't recognize, to this lovely baby. My baby! I felt so many emotions warring within me. I was dumbstruck; words refused to make themselves heard.

Sameer broke the reverie with a wisecrack "It's the hormonal changes mummy, something we have to live with for the next few months".

"Shut up Sameer, I understand Simran" saying this, *dadi* hugged me while I simply cried.

10th May

Today's was a big bag of surprises. The day took an unexpected positive as it unfolded. It started with me preparing breakfast. Pushpa *Bhua* had asked for *dosas*, *bread pulav*, grilled sandwiches and mango *sandesh*. I couldn't fathom where she was going to stuff it all in. No wonder she is the size she is. Kept grumbling and muttering (silently as I couldn't risk being audible for Radha *maasi* and Raju were beside me helping me prepare). To be fair, they were doing most of the work while I was supervising them. I then went to answer the doorbell and saw Pushpa *Bhua* sporting a wide grin. And then before I had time to react there was a loud shout of SURPRISE! The next instant Ravi and Simar appeared carrying a huge teddy bear between them. After a brief and silent pause (I was too taken back to even react), I hugged my siblings and warm greetings were exchanged. It took quite some time for my excitement to settle down.

"Simi you have to thank Pushpa *bhua* for this lovely surprise". I raised my eyebrows questioningly at Sameer who carried on, "She had it all arranged. Not only did she suggest that we invite them here but also convinced a very reluctant mummy that this was the best time to send you to Kolkata. She has been planning this from the day she arrived and had threatened us with dire consequences if we spilt the beans. Now you understand how surprised I was when you spoke about travelling to Kolkata to Sudha aunty. For a split second I thought that you somehow managed to get a whiff of our plan. I was petrified about *Bhua* killing me for letting you in on to our little secret". This sure left me speechless. What was I supposed to say or think? Here I kept cribbing about her even before she arrived; there she was going to great lengths just to bring a smile to my face. This always happens to me. Just when I think that I know someone very well, turns out my opinion was wrong. At that moment you can imagine how small and petty I felt. I guess it is human nature that when we have preconceived notions of dislike about someone we actually seek to only highlight the negatives. I always thought that everything she said was wrong, all she did was unnecessary and there was nothing worthwhile to learn from her experience. Today I stood corrected. Now I believed in the positive effect of the chants and mantras she asked me to listen to, the ill effects of the junk food that I had started gorging on and the benefits of walking and working that she regularly coaxed me into doing. I had to make it up to her and apologize for my past behavior (not that I had let it show on my face ever).

"Simi you have lost a lot of weight. I hardly recognized you without your chubby cheeks", said my dear brother Ravi. His infuriatingly bad jokes about my weight however were not so dear. He used to always tease me about being chubby as a kid. And the nickname *Fats* sort of hung around long after I shed my baby fat. He on the other hand was always on the lean side, though lately he's been working out which along with the protein supplements show in his well-developed physique. With *Nana*'s brown eyes and dark hair, and *Nani*'s fair complexion and a perfect aquiline nose, he did look very handsome and at 5 11" he's turns many heads! Many of my friends had a major crush on him and some even went to the extent of flirting with him, which he completely ignored. Having completed his M.B.A from the University of Michigan, he has finally joined dad's business of manufacturing and trading in tyres. "So you really cooked all this? Well, well, well, is this not surprising Simar? Must inform mummy that her daughter is finally capable of cooking well. If I hadn't seen this with my own eyes, I wouldn't have believed it to be true".

Ravi just doesn't know when to stop. And his big mouth was

blurting all this is front of your *dadi*. Now she probably knew what a big *Kaamchor* I was. But yes it is true; I don't even lift a finger when I am in *Nani's* place.

"Simi, my baby sister. Can't believe my little sister is going to become a mummy". 'Little? Baby? Right. I was only 13 months younger than him but he still feels he has the license to call me little. "Ravi please stop teasing her. Now Simi you just sit down and relax and I will help clean up".

That was my sweet sister Simar. An absolute angel (except when she was really young). We are two years apart and as kids fought like wild cats over the smallest of things. *Nani -nana* had a tough time with the three of us always at each other's throats. They would try to mediate between us, but for a little while. As soon as they stopped, our *Tom and Jerryesque* battles would start all over again (much to the anguish of *nani*).

Simar looks a splitting image of mom. She stands tall at 5' 8", a good three inches taller than me. Sharp nose, dark eyes, long black wavy hair, fair complexion and a cute smile. We do not share much of a resemblance (she looks like *nani* and I take after *nana*). She is an absolute cleanliness nut and that had been a real blessing in my younger days. Whatever the mess I left behind, she would've it straightened up in a matter of minutes. She would sort out my really messy cupboards and do my share of the work around the house all because my benchmarks for cleanliness did not meet her high standards. How I missed her when I got married. How was I supposed to keep the entire house sparkling clean without her by my side? I miss all our lengthy conversations, hours of gossiping, leching at guys, shopping together and other sisterly activities. She has always been my best friend in whom I can not only confide, but also depend on, for sensible advice.

Both Simar and Ravi were here and now it was party time!!!

But first I thanked Pushpa *bhua* for everything. She likes to retire early (early to bed and early to rise) so I headed straight to her room. "Thank you *Bhua* for going out of the way to make me happy. It was really sweet on your part. You have always been taking care of me and in every instruction of yours, there's only loving concern for me. Today I know that you want only the best for me. Thank you not just for this surprise; which I promise I will never forget but for everything".

She smiled, patted my head and shut the door. She, as you would be aware by now, isn't overt in her displays of affection.

14th May

Had no time to write during the last few days which just slipped by. I had plenty of fun and spent hours laughing, courtesy Ravi. He would often have me in splits and I was forced to beg him to stop as my stomach would start to ache with all the laughing. Tried out many new restaurants. Indulged in a lot of shopping (my family's favorite past-time), played a lot of board games which would invariably end in mock fights. Ravi would not allow me to make up words which did not exist in the dictionary and refused to lose to me just because I was pregnant. Yes baby, he can be pretty heartless at times.

I treated them to a lavish experience of a Gold Class theater when we watched a couple of movies. This hadn't yet appeared in their city and both of them were totally enthralled by the experience. Long drives became mandatory during the nights, with Simar wanting to have ice-cream from a particular parlor far from home. She had more or less taken over the kitchen which allowed me to take a well- deserved break.

Yesterday Ravi and Sameer prepared breakfast for all of us

(which curiously enough, was served during lunch time). The *idlis* were a little lumpy, the *sambhar* bland and the *chutney* too spicy. The only saving grace was the sandwiches (they were pretty innovative with Mexican bean filling) and we gladly chomped it down. But of course we showered the cooks with a lot of praise and lavished them with our compliments while telling them that we hoped tha they would try their hand at cooking a lot more often (not really). Your dad has a lot to learn in this field, he's yet to make even a decent cup of tea! But he does look real cute in my pink apron.

Pushpa *Bhua* left yesterday night. Guess what? I am actually missing her.

17th May

Had a big fight with Sameer today! He happened to see my diary lying around and managed to read a few pages, before I snatched it away from him and sort of hurt him on the chin in the process. A lengthy argument followed. You see, he did not know that I was writing a diary and now he obviously wanted to read it, which I did not allow him to. This diary is for your eyes only. It is a mother-baby thing. Something which only the two of us can share.

"Nothing is supposed to remain a secret between us. And since it is for my child I have every right in the world to read it. Please just give me ten minutes and I will take a quick sneak peek" implored Sameer.

Did I relent? Of course not! Only you can read it and I intend for it to remain that way. Ravi actually had to intervene in our argument for it was about to turn ugly. I might have actually punched Sameer's face had Ravi not pulled him away on time. I again blame this behavior of mine on hormonal changes, but I still laugh every time I recall his shocked expression. He was absolutely dumbfounded seeing me get so aggressive. Ravi was totally composed as he had not only witnessed similar behavior, but had in fact actively participated in similar fights during our childhood. We fought furiously as kids! Fist fights, kicking and hair pulling; I would pull his hair so hard that he would often cry out in pain. However, having said that, I request you not to behave in such a manner with your sibling (as and when you have one). Please don't drive me mad like we drove our mother. Sameer continued to sulk and mope about and did not talk for quite some time.

Packing is over. I am travelling light (only a couple of suitcases) for I intend to shop out there. Ravi kept grumbling about the weight. "Your suitcases weight almost as much as you Simi. What on earth have you stuffed them with, boulders?" "Ravi stop cribbing, these are just basic necessities". Wonder why Ravi and Sameer gave each other such wry knowing looks.

18th May

Landed in Kolkata. I felt like I had entered a furnace. The heat seemed to engulf me as I left the airport. The five minute wait, for the car to arrive was torturous. *Nani* came to pick me up with a box of heavenly baked goodies. Gave her a quick hug before diving in the air conditioned bliss of the car. One pastry, one slice of pizza and a sandwich later, began conversing with her.

"Now no more *bachpana*, you must take care of yourself. Only then will the baby grow properly. Be very careful of what you eat. Don't eat outside food especially from street vendors. Nowadays you hear of so many cases of food poisoning". "But mom you just got me food from outside." "Just this once. O.K?"

Right! As if she actually expected me not to indulge in *pucchkas and jhaal Moori.* Mom is pretty easy going except when it comes to eating. No gluttony, no junk food, no unhealthy snacking, no skipping milk and meals etc. I on the other hand beg to totally differ with her definition of good eating habits. You can't even begin to guess the number of arguments we have had over my dietary habits, but why am I telling you all this? I seriously hope you do not take after me in this regard. Please do be like your dad who is a very non-fussy eater.

It was a little upsetting saying bye to Sameer, but I cheered up as soon as I landed here. There is so much to do. Catch up with friends, lunches with cousins, dinner outings with relatives, lots of reading and stuffing myself with the famous delicacies of this city. Now if only I could get Bangalore's weather here. Throughout the journey back, both Ravi and Simar tried to grab a puff or pastry for themselves but I would have none of it. It was all mine!

Met *nana* in the evening. I am his absolute favorite. His little princess actually. Sameer always blames him for pampering and spoiling me in my childhood, the consequences of which he has to suffer now. I think he is just jealous that he was not fussed over so much.

Age seems to finally be showing on dad. A few fine wrinkles have appeared on his forehead. Some white strands are now visible in his otherwise thick, black hair. Despite all this he still looks much younger than his 51 years. I was so glad to see him! Dinner was my all-time favorite, *Pav Bhaji.* Chatted with *nani* & *nana* while Simar did all the unpacking.

30th May

Time sure flies! Seems all the days have just zipped by me. Morning would start only by 10 o' clock and that too because *nani* would force me to get up so that I could eat something. It is difficult to get up early if you sleep by 1 or 2 in the night. Had lots of get-togethers. Almost the whole of *nana's* family is based here (one sister and three brothers). Both of *nani's* sisters are here too, only a brother stays in Chennai. Most of my cousins are about my age and we meet often.

Priya and Gaurav are the ones I am closest to. Together we were a tiresome bunch of pranksters (most of those pranks were harmless) as kids and were often addressed (in jest) as the "terrible threesome".

One downside about being a *marwari* in Kolkata is the endless socializing. Almost everyday there is at least one function or get together to compulsorily attend. Initially one enjoys it, but it slowly begins to wear you down with its monotony and you soon start dreading having to step out. And then the excuses start. Mine are now verging on the highly innovative. Like the one I gave Reema aunty, *nani's* cousin who had invited me for her granddaughter's 3rd birthday party. Like I wanted to waste my precious Sunday amongst a bunch of mewling three year olds while having juice spilt over my new dress. So I politely but firmly turned down the invite saying, "aunty I would have loved to come but some property papers need to be signed urgently. Sameer's lawyer is flying in with them and is in a hurry. I will need to be at the airport itself to do all the work. The timing clashes with your party and unfortunately it is at the other end of the city. So there is absolutely no way I will be able to make it."

I congratulated myself for coming up with such a brilliant

excuse and sat down to read *Kane and Able* by *Jeffery Archer* (a most versatile author). I hadn't gone past a hundred pages when *nani* returned in a pretty foul mood from the party.

"Reema didi was really upset with your behavior. Why could you not simply say that you were tired and couldn't make it, rather than cook up such a tall story? You didn't even bother informing me about it. When she questioned me about what time you were to return from the airport, I answered that she must be mistaken as there were no plans of you meeting anyone and you were relaxing at home. She now claims to be very hurt by your rude behavior. I tried to cover up, and said that you probably forgot to tell me about the whole episode, but by then the cat was already out of the bag."

Me, my big mouth, and my brilliant ideas. Not only was mom upset but I was also sure to be in Reema aunty's bad books for a long time to come.

Barring this one incident, so far the days have been going great. The news of my pregnancy has now spread like wildfire amongst all my relatives. Someone or the other keeps sending across their own special signature dish almost everyday. Additionally, more often than not, my cousins are over to help me eat these large portions which would otherwise be impossible for me to finish on my own.

7th June

Met my school friends for lunch yesterday. There are no friends like school friends. The strong bonds survive the test of time. Whatever time has passed, we still meet and chat like we've never ever been out of touch. There is so much to talk about, so much to catch up with. We discussed teachers, bitched about the most popular girl in class, reminisced about the oily, spicy canteen food and sighed over the times when our waists were size 24. We discussed our crushes and heartbreaks over chocolate cupcakes (without blushing about them anymore). We went gaga over each other's achievements, talked about future plans, discussed current love interests and basically relived our teenage days all over again. The hot topic of discussion for today was Aparna's engagement ceremony which is to take place tomorrow. Most of my friends are yet to settle down and are presently concentrating on their careers. I guess I got married when I was a bit too young. Who ties the knot at 21 in this day and age? I was yet to finish my final year exams, which were to take place three months later, when I tied the knot. Sameer used to tutor me during the evenings and it was only with his help, that I managed to get a first class degree. He even came down to be with me during my exams and was my pillar of support throughout.

Let me get back to matters at hand, I had to decide what to wear for Aparna's engagement. I also can't decide on a gift for her. Should I gift a silver photo frame or a show piece?

Additionally, it also happens to be the fifth month of my pregnancy! Still no sign of any bulge. Have put on a few kilos and I am back to my old weight. I can see myself becoming overweight, if I remain here longer. The food here is to die for. Bengali sweets are heavenly and I cannot seem to get enough of *rasgullas, gulab jamuns* and *sandeshs*. The *club kachori* served in all the popular breakfast places is another everyday must for me. The *samosas* deserve a mention too. Simar often jokes about food being my sole agenda for visiting the city of joy. I treated you every day to a scoop of cookies and cream at my favorite ice-cream joint.

11th June

Yippee!!! Sameer is coming down tomorrow. I am so happy. Said he missed me terribly (hope it is true).

"I miss hearing you talk endlessly about nothing. Miss the fights you start for no particular reason. Miss you hogging the entire blanket, leaving me to freeze during the nights. Miss your calls asking me to come home early so we can step out to grab a bite. You know, I have actually lost weight because I now don't have to eat out everyday?" I had to cut him short before his list of very unromantic reasons for missing me started to grow longer. I guess he was just kidding (he better be).

Today I had gone to see a prospective bride for Gaurav. Since I am his favorite cousin, I got the honour of accompanying his parents on this auspicious quest. Another reason was that he wanted somebody his age to assess the girl and judge if she would be compatible with him. I didn't mind it, as going along with the potential groom's family meant a lot of *Khatirdari*, which simply put meant that we would receive royal treatment! Arranged marriages are a very long and lengthy process. First a distant (probably) relative will present a prospective alliance with a suitable boy/girl from particular place. Profiles are exchanged while background information is ferreted out from all possible sources. If all these hurdles are cleared, then the boy's parents see the girl and vice-versa. If approved, then the boy and girl are finally allowed to meet in the company of relatives who keep tabs on their every move. If you are lucky, you get to meet a couple of times (always accompanied by a relative) before having to say yes to the match. Sameer and I too got married in a similar manner.

I didn't think that this girl was the one for Gaurav however. She was as tall if not taller than my 5 feet 5 inch cousin. Also she didn't know how to cook, nor was she keen on learning. I could sense aunty mentally crossing out her name after that remark. We enjoyed their hospitality, ate at their expense, spoke and laughed with them before passing the message through the common relative that 'we will think about it'. This is the politest form of refusal ever invented. You can't be openly rude so you use euphemisms to convey the message. Will give Gaurav all the details later, but first wanted to plan some sort of surprise for Sameer.

Simar decided to bake a cake with *Welcome Jiju* written on it. *Nani* went all out with the culinary preparations. Wish you could've gone over the spread. It was as extensive as a buffet spread. Ha! Ha! Sameer was going to put on all the lost weight that he claimed to have shed, and if *nani* had her way, then it would probably be a lot more than just that. For my part I decided not to argue with him while he was here; nothing will surprise him more than that.

Went out for dinner with Aparna and her fiancé along with a bunch of other friends. He was treating all of us at a Barbecue themed restaurant. Her engagement was very extravagant to put it mildly. She had invited most of our classmates and it was pretty nostalgic to see quite a few of them there. She looked pretty (the beautician has to be commended as she is not a great looker) in her pink *ghagra* heavily done up with crystals. Too bad Akshad (her fiancé) did not visit the parlour for he looked decidedly in need of a facelift. Our entire gang together went on stage during the engagement to congratulate the couple. 'What a perfect couple', 'a nice pair', 'made for each other' and the other such clichés were freely served up. Today's dinner was probably the last outing with my friends for this trip, because I will have to accompany a very grouchy Sameer on lunches and dinners from tomorrow at all my relative's places. Such is tradition if the SIL comes to town. Your close relatives will invite him over for at least one meal (your dad though absolutely hates that). Let me see him try to talk himself out of that!

16th June

Leaving tomorrow morning for Bangalore. *Nani* keeps shedding a few tears every now and then while Sameer keeps trying to comfort her. She still cries every time I leave. I guess it is natural for a mother to feel upset at being separated from her children. "Are those tears of joy mummy? Aren't you glad that she is finally leaving?" Sameer and his lame jokes. He enjoyed himself thoroughly however. My visit to the City of Joy was about to end and barring for a couple of times that I threw up, it had gone off really well. I laughed, shopped, spoke endlessly with friends and cousins, spend a lot of quality time with *nani* and *nana*, relished the food, lazed around and now it is was with a very heavy heart that I had to leave. Ravi promises to let me win all the games the next time I came (like I believe he would) and all Simar did was talk about how cool it will be to become a *maasi.* We kept talking about how life would change once you arrived. I am waiting for that beautiful moment when you will be in my arms and complete my world.

24th June

Back to the same boring and monotonous schedule. Get up and help about in the kitchen, read, sleep in the afternoon, a walk in a nearby park (yup, have started walking for 30 minutes everyday) rounded off with normal *roti* and *subzi* meals (Sameer has strictly asked me to lay off outside food as I have apparently had more than enough of it in Kolkata, and for once I think he is right). Will go to Sudha aunty for a checkup. After consulting with her, will get my fifth month ultrasound done. Sameer and mummy are waiting for it. Sameer always talks about me being so lucky to have you grow within me and feel all your movements. Gosh! It just slipped my mind, mentioning the movements earlier. So like me to keep rambling on about all the small details and forget the big picture. The movements are the best part of the pregnancy. At least for now. I have been warned that the kicks you are going to unleash on me in the coming months will not be too pleasurable. The first movements which began at the onset of the second trimester, were initially very faint. Felt as if a butterfly was fluttering about in the stomach. Slowly they graduated to gentle brushes. How good they felt. They assured me of you being safe and sound. Now as the weeks kept passing by, you make your presence felt in a much more prominent manner. Your dad loves to place his hands on my tummy, just to feel you move about within me. At times you oblige with more than necessary, while you disappoint on other occasions. He talks to you everyday. Honestly speaking, I do get a little tired of hearing the same words being repeated.

He does care a lot for us and has gone to great lengths to ensure our health and happiness. There is nothing he won't do. All I have to do is ask. You know there are times when I don't even have to do that. He just sort of reads my mind and before I even ask, it is done! He is lavishing even more attention on me now than during our days of courtship. Those days were a completely different story and would love to share them with you someday.

Brownies' have been playing on my mind for quite sometime. Craving for them. Must ask Sameer to pick up some from Barista.

26th June

You are going to be a very hyperactive child. I have already seen signs of it. Today we had to undergo the ultrasound thrice, as you refused to keep still. Just kept tossing and turning. The measurement could not be taken the first two times. On both those occasions, I was told to eat some more and come after half an hour. I didn't mind the eating part. The hospital had a very good canteen and the meals served there was really good. I washed it all down with a large glass of orange juice. The *parathas* which mummy had packed for me were very conveniently forgotten in the car. The visit to Dr. Sudha had gone very well. My weight now has gone up marginally but was informed that it should now start increasing at a much more rapid rate. The B.P was normal and the pregnancy is progressing just fine. She asked me to now start attending Lamaze classes.

"They really help you in understanding exactly what to expect. Also you will learn breathing techniques which will benefit both you and the baby." Iron and calcium pills were to be continued and my water intake had to be at least two litres a day. This was really difficult, firstly the weather of Bangalore is so cool and pleasant, you hardly ever feel thirsty. Wherever I try to drink more than a few sips of water, I just can't seem to keep it down. It therefore doesn't make sense to drink half a glass and then proceed to puke out everything I had eaten in the last two hours, along with that very glass of water. Anyway, third time lucky it was when you finally seemed to have gone to sleep (I guess you tired yourself out) and the technician was able to complete the ultrasound. I just love to hear your heartbeat, without overdoing it; the machine makes it sound like a galloping horse. *Dadi* missed the ultrasound today. She had to visit one of her cousins who had undergone a bypass surgery.

You had definitely grown in size and your features were getting better defined. Each time I saw your image I felt more excited than ever.

5th July

I am in Coorg. A surprise holiday. Planned and executed by none other than your dad. At seven in the morning he asked me to get ready for a good breakfast and we are off in a jiffy. So lost I was in my non-shop chatter, that I did not notice that we weren't on our usual route. A good while later I came to the realization that we weren't heading to our regular breakfast pitstop. Sameer told me then, that he wanted to try a different place and because it was meant to be a surprise, I shouldn't ask anymore questions. Ha!!! Big mistake; telling me not to question things was the easiest way to arouse my curiosity. I nagged him no end after that, but he did not relent. Suresh *bhaiya* too seemed in cahoots with Sameer and kept mum despite my incessant prodding. Pretending to be angry, I turned the other way and looked outside. We were now nearing Mysore road. What exactly was Sameer planning? Made my peace and let the surprise remain a surprise (for once). I slept through the entire journey on his lap (feigning a back ache). At about 10 we reached a very popular eatery located about fifty kilometers on the main Mysore road. I woke up, stretched and did a few neck exercises. We had to wait as it was a little crowded, but the breakfast was awesome. The *kadabu idlis* were one of a kind and the *set dosa* melted in my mouth. I skipped the coffee and settled for a juice instead. Sameer likes his coffee extra strong without sugar.

"Now let us head home". Sameer said, while turning towards the car. "You made me travel for two hours just to have breakfast.

Is this your idea of surprise? You have to be kidding me". Obviously, I was outraged.

"But just about 10 min back you were raving about the idlis".

"I didn't know that I had to travel four hours just to eat them when I said that".

He laughed and coaxed me back to sleep. I knew that there had to be more to come and readily complied. A nice nap of about two hours had me refreshed. Sameer was glad when I woke up. "Thank God!" He said trying to feel his feet. "My legs have gone to sleep, and my poor back, let's not even go there."

I just rested my head for two hours on his lap and he creates a scene. Men! Pffft.

"Where are we heading?" I asked ignoring his whining.

"Just another hour and you will know."

"We are obviously going for a few days, or a couple of nights at least" I hopefully asked of him.

"Ask no questions and you will be told no lies," replied the wise guy.

In about an hour's time I did figure out. I sat upright through the remainder of the journey to indicate my displeasure at his complaints and despite him apologizing did not lie down. We were now heading towards Coorg.

The car was moving at moderate speed. You know how your dad feels about driving fast with his pregnant wife. We finally reached our destination in 6 and bit hours, but on reaching the journey's end I had no reason to complain.

We were in Orange County - one of the most beautiful resorts in our country, and during the coming days I got to figure out why.

8th July

With Sameer, I can only expect the very best. The resort was amazing. The property was huge and seemed endless when you walked around. There is so much well maintained greenery all around. The foliage was perfectly trimmed. The staff were extremely polite and were wonderfully dedicated to keeping us happy, which reflected in their "Yes I can" badges. They were highly efficient and looked to make you comfortable all the while. We had a pool villa booked for a whole week. That meant that I was celebrating my second wedding anniversary here, yippee! The rooms were built in the style of traditional cottages. The place is divided into tents, regular rooms and pool villas. We were told that *Aishwarya Rai*, *Amitabh Bacchan* and *Vivek Oberoi* had filmed here for one of their movies; the best bit though was that the pool villa where we were staying was the one where the BIG B WAS PUT UP. Wow!! Wow and more wow!! Can it get bigger than this? The biggest legend of Indian cinema stayed in the very same room that I am in? Just can't wait to tell this to everyone. But that would have to wait as there is no network here. You can only make calls from room phones, which is a blessing in disguise for Sameer because he needed to get away from being on call all the time and the continuous badgering of his managers for various nitty-gritties.

Dadi and Sameer had done all the packing and it was an extremely good job too. My clothes, different shoes, shades, medicines, cosmetics, my camera; everything was there. Plus there was a separate hand bag filled with dry snacks and a few books too! *Dadi* does think of everything. The bedroom was very spacious and was connected to the living room, and a private, open air pool was accessible from both these rooms. The best part is that it has two bathrooms and I don't need to nag Sameer asking him to hurry up. The buffet spread was good but better still they actually made a few dishes on request just for me. Room service wasn't something they encouraged but they relented in my case as a pregnant lady deserved some special concessions.

The *ayurvedic* massage center here is one of a kind. The massage rooms are very spacious and have a soothing ambience. Before a massage you are given a choice music you would like to listen to. Then both the therapists say a small, catchy prayer. I could not enjoy all their famous massages, because of my condition and had to content myself with *shirodhara* which is a head massage. Sameer was all praises however, for the *sarvangadhara* massage where five therapists massage you simultaneously and a lot of oil is used. I have to come back to experience it.

Today, my 6th month has commenced. Time sure runs by. Still waiting for the bulge to become much more prominent.

I skipped the nature walk which was to last for a few hours since it wasn't recommended for a pregnant woman. Instead, I decided to relax and read. Reading is something I have been fond of even as a child. Started with fairytales, and then moved on to *Famous Five* and *Secret Seven*, before graduating to *Agatha Christie, Sherlock Holmes* and other classics. After marriage, all I have read are best sellers in fiction. It is one hobby I wish you would passionately cultivate. Reading opens doors to a world fueled by imagination. Good books not only will improve your vocabulary, but also help you to think freely and imaginatively. They put us through situations which we might not actually face in reality. Lastly the best part is that you are never lonely when you have a book along with you. *Marcus Tullius Cicero* has rightly said, *"A room without books is like a body without a soul."* Read *Love Story* by *Eric Segal* for the nth time lazing on the hammock. Not a very good idea though, given my mood swings. Got so sentimental that I couldn't stop crying.

10th July

This anniversary was very memorable. Breakfast was served in bed. The staff presented us with a bouquet. A quick dip in the pool followed. It was quick, because it started raining. It had been raining on and off which made it generally chilly afterwards. We also need to walk slowly because the ground can get slippery after a shower. Spent the afternoon indoors while feasting on a Chinese lunch. In the evening we participated in lot of games by the bonfire. Back in the villa room I was surprised to see the entire room decorated with flowers and the pool was surrounded by candles. It was so perfect. Dinner was served by our private butler. Then late into night Sameer presented me with a rose. Inside the rose was a beautiful 3 carat solitaire set on a gold band. Inside the band was inscribed "We are forever." He slipped it on my finger and said,

"You have bought immense joy to my life. Your madness keeps me sane, I love the way you bring out the best in me. I will cherish our love forever. From the day you walked into my life, I have experienced love the kind we only read about. I fell in love the moment I first laid my eyes on you. You looked so beautiful. The wind was sweeping the waist length hair across your face. The blue dress highlighted your fair complexion. Your large black eyes were nervously following me around. Your sharp nose, the high cheekbones, the luscious pink lips, your slender figure; everything had me completely smitten then and now. You complete me. Simran I can proudly say that I am very lucky to have you in my life. Promise me that you will always remain the way you are. Nothing about you should ever change. The way you smile, your tantrums, the gleam in your eyes, your mischievous pranks, your beautiful laughter which never fails to brighten even the gloomiest of days.

In my eyes you are as perfect as perfect can be. Happy anniversary my love and may there be many more down the road. My love for you is eternally enduring."

Guess what? I hadn't even bought him a gift!!

12th July

Was disappointed to head back home (I always feel that way after every vacation). It was a perfect holiday, one I shall always remember. We bought identical T-shirts, lots of spices (Coorg is famous for them) and caps. I promised to return with you here soon. The journey back was uneventful (wasn't very talkative) and I listened to a lot of golden oldies. Sameer is crazy about them and we have an extensive playlist containing the works of *Mukesh, Kishore Kumar*, *Lata Mangeshkar* and *Mohammad Rafi*. I slept most of time, which gave Sameer a reason to again to crib about his poor feet which had gone to sleep. This time, I did not bother reacting.

Dadi and *dada* were waiting to welcome me back home. "The house is so quiet without you. I really missed you".

"What about me mom? Your son. Your flesh and blood".

"Stop being melodramatic Sameer. I suppose we missed you too, but Simran was missed more". Sameer pretended to sulk upon hearing this. There are just four of us here as a family and even if one person isn't around then it does tend to feel incomplete, but that is only until you arrive. Then I am sure that there won't ever be a dull moment around.

20th July

Have you ever hated someone so much that it changes the very definition of the word hatred? You'll meet all kinds of people in life. You will love some, agree with others, dislike few and maybe even hate a person or two, but there will also be those rare occasions when your dislike for someone transcends hatred. I too have come across one such character that evokes intense hatred in me, the likes of which I never believed myself capable of. I am referring to none other than Tara *mami*. She is your *dadi*'s brother's wife and Sameer's *mami*. She is a perfect ***** (in interest of decency, I shall leave it to your imagination to fill in the necessary words).

Nobody likes her. Let me rephrase that, none of us can even tolerate her. We have to force ourselves to be civil to her. She had come over for a week to shop for her daughter's wedding! Can you believe it, a person from Mumbai coming to shop in Bangalore? Our city has some of the finest silk products, but other than that, what can it offer which Mumbai, the fashion hub of our country, can't? She had planned to shop for a whole week! Let me describe her in detail, she is short and portly. Her dark skin has a lot of blemishes and a large part of her face is covered with freckles. In contrast *dadi's* soft rounded face looks the very epitome of homely perfection especially on her motherly build which is rounded off with her lovely waist length hair, which is always braided. Let's leave the appearance aside as looks are God gifted and not much can be done about it until and unless you are ready to go under the surgeon's knife. It's our character that defines who we are and hers is of the worst kind.

Yesterday morning she informed us that she would be arriving by the evening flight. Of course she didn't deem it necessary to notify us well beforehand. It seems that she thinks that there isn't anything important happening in our lives and she can drop in whenever she pleases. In a way it was good that we did not receive prior notification, else we would have gone into depression earlier. *Dadi* personally supervised the cleaning of her room and kept into account all her food preferences while preparing dinner. But did she appreciate it? Fat chance.

"Why did you have to make dinner? Hasn't Simran yet managed to find her way about the kitchen? When on earth will you learn to be a good MIL? If you give them so much of leeway, then one day they are going make you dance to their tunes."

"Simran does her fair share of household chores. We only insist on her not exerting herself more than necessary as she has been advised plenty of rest by the doctor" stated dear *dada* jumping to my rescue.

"Girls today behave like such dainty darlings. Lift a finger and they are easily tired. So what if she is pregnant? Did we not work during our nine months? You people have it so easy. During our time, we worked round the clock. We did not have servants and machines. Our hands were all the automation we ever had. Aruna, you have five servants. Why you are spoiling her so?"

"That is because her family cares about her comfort and well-being and we can address those needs in style" retorted *dada.*

Ouch! That comment would have stung a lot, as Rajesh *mama* is not very well off. The colour drained from her face and mummy tried to change the topic by discussing about the marriage preparations. She pretended not to have heard the comment but I am sure *dada* would be heading the list of people who she would bad mouth later. I felt deeply touched by the loving concern my FIL had for me. To get on the wrong side of Tara *mami* was equivalent to putting your hand in a hornet's nest. There was no telling how many times you would be stung.

Today was mainly reserved for snide rants. She started (only after papa and Sameer left, for she did not want to be admonished like yesterday) her tirade after breakfast. Her target for the day was Mona *mami*. She is your *dadi*'s younger brother Vipul *mama's* wife and both the *derani* and *jethani* could not possibly be more opposite. She is a darling (and appears all the more so in contrast to her co-sister). Vipul *mama* has a successful real estate business, but his wife has no airs either about her husband's wealth or her good looks. Her friendly disposition makes her a favourite with all her relatives. Tara *mami* had just spent twenty days in Delhi at Vipul mama's residence. Mona *mami* had assisted her in shopping for Palak's (Tara *mami's* daughter) trousseau and how is she repayed for her kindness?

"Mona is very pretentious. She is always talking about how much Vipul earns. A rather intolerable attitude. No respect for elders or any etiquette. If money makes you such a monster then I am better off without it". Those twenty days were a real pain. I tell you."

Of course we didn't believe a word of what she said. The morning turned into afternoon and soon faded into dusk. All we did during that time was listen to her cruel accusations. Now why wasn't she shopping? Was that not the very reason she dropped in unannounced like a bad storm upon us?

25th July

As kids we read fairy tales and believe them, but when we grow up, we view them as silly stories. However, if we closely look around, characters from these stories are actually a reflection of the reality in front of us. They are just packaged differently. Each girl is a princess in her own right and is on the lookout of her prince charming. The prince might not slay dragons or own castles, but from the girl's perspective he's a prince. Parents are kings and queens and our godfathers qualify as our guardian angels. So too with wicked witches or cruel step mothers. They too can be found, but without the accompanying props. My advice to you my child, would be to stay as far away as possible from such people. They can only spread evil. Be true to yourself and make sure that that such people are unable to influence you. Choose your friends and companions very wisely. When the character of a man is not clear, then people look at the friends he keeps.

Tara *mami* is the personification of the wicked witch stereotype. She must have tried many times to poison *dadi*'s mind against me. She would frequently be whispering something maliciously to *dadi*, stopping suddenly on seeing me. Your *dadi* knows better than pay her any heed, but she can be pretty persuasive which makes me uneasy.

Dadi wanted to plan my *Saadh Purai* which is a small ceremony done to celebrate the completion of seven months of your first pregnancy. But she decided to wait for *kansmami* to leave before the preparations began. Anyways there's no rush. I still have two weeks to go before my seventh month commences.

After ensuring that *mami* was safely tucked in her room and sound asleep (her snores could be heard in the hall) we all sat together in *dadi-dada*'s room.

"Thank God she is leaving tomorrow. Can't stand the sight of her face. She is like the vamp of most of the serials that you watch Aruna." Such strong sentiments in plain words could only come from *dada*.

"She too feels the same way about you. Just yesterday she was telling me that I had rushed into the marriage and could have got someone better than you" laughed *dadi*.

"She even said that Sameer deserved better" I wailed.

Sameer the wiseguy had to say something to that, "perhaps we misjudged her. Maybe she is not so bad after all. She has correctly judged my dire situation". I pretended to be hurt by Sameer's comment (though I knew he was jesting).

"How dare she comment about my daughter? It is Simran who deserves someone far better than Sameer. Ask her to find anyone who can measure upto her," (ok, I'll admit that this was a tad too much to digest, even for my inflated ego). Yes I am *dada's* pet! He just will not hear anything against me and is always ready to offer his unconditional support. Sameer should have known better than to open his mouth in front of him.

We all then played a few hands of bridge and I had to keep adjusting my pillow all throughout, to provide relief to my aching back.

26th July

Hip! Hip! Hooray! She's finally left. Smiles are back on everyone's faces, especially the poor servants. They can now breathe a sigh of relief. She was mean to them too while she was here. Never a kind word for them or a compassionate glance. She also stopped me from helping Sudhir, the watchman's son with his English.

"Your daughter-in-law has lost her mind, but does better sense not prevail in you Aruna? How can you allow her to mingle with the children of the servants of the house? And why is she trying to educate them? Just because these people receive an education, they no longer want to work as servants. She is one of the reasons why people like me have a tough time getting servants. Out you go...." A crying eight year old Sudhir was unceremoniously herded out.

Today though he was back with his books and I helped him

in constructing a few simple sentences. Tara *mami* was a real terror. Some people are just born mean. There were no major incidents in her life that I know of which could account for her lack of empathy.

Why does *dadi* have to put up with her nonsense? She's always worried that she might offend someone. She never wants to be considered a bad person. That's the reason she keeps bending her back over to please such petty minded people. What right did Pushpa *bhua* have to tell her how to run her household (however well-meaning her intentions might have been)? How on earth could Tara *mami* criticize her husband and *bahu*? Instead of putting them in their rightful places, *dadi* always tried to make peace with such people, which obviously didn't go down very well with me. If I had the authority I would have long shown her the door. Such people deserve nothing better. Also, if mummy thought that *mami* would thank her and praise her in front of other relatives then she was in for a shock. Did she not see the way Mona *mami* was crucified despite going all out to help her? And the funny part is that despite taking her all around the city, all she ended up buying was just a silk *saree.*

7th August

Celebrated your *dadi*'s birthday along with the commencement of my seventh month. Arranged a surprise party for her. I sent her for a complete body massage, facial and pedicure at a reputed Spa. Asked *dada* to pick her up in the afternoon for a movie. In the meantime I had the hall decorated, supervised the caterers and send reminders to her friends (she has a lot of them) whom I had secretly been calling the whole of last week, which meant a lot of calls. My long anticipated bulge has finally appeared. All in a matter of a few weeks. This development was also accompanied by difficulty in walking and quite a few ugly stretch marks. Now how did this happen? No matter how many tubes of vitamin E I used up on my stomach, it just wouldn't work. I find these marks quite disgusting, but Sameer thinks that they look cute. I know he is bluffing.

Suresh *bhaiya* arrived with the cake. It was heart shaped and I was tempted to write 49 on it but then thought the better of it. No woman whatever her age maybe, likes to be reminded about it. After all why do we frequent parlours, try out many types of cosmetics, have all sorts of ghastly face packs on, walk, jog, workout and do yoga? We do so just to appear younger! To have people exclaim "you cannot be, you definitely look at least 10 years younger" and "you've got to be kidding me". Therefore no sense in having 49 candles on the cake. Cannot risk rubbing my '*sasumd*' the wrong way. You too please make a mental note of it. Let's make it an unspoken rule on my birthdays. Leave the candles out. The guests started arriving. Thankfully I didn't have to address them by their names for I do not know most of them. Just aunty and uncle will do. I am so glad that it didn't rain today. It had been pouring continuously every day. By early evening, most of the sixty odd guests had arrived and I told *dada* to then make his entry with *dadi*. Boy was she surprised! For a few moments she stood there with her mouth wide open before she could finally compose herself.

She thanked me and then quickly started interacting with all her friends. She just loves to socialize and rarely misses any get-togethers. The party went on till about an hour before midnight and was a big hit! However I was completely exhausted by the time the last guest left. Sameer told me to rest while he settled the bills. There are no gifts for *dadi* to open (we strictly do not accept gifts and I made sure I let this be known to all the invitees) except the one presented by Sameer and I. Ok, *dada* too. He always asks me to pick up something I deem suitable. She absolutely loved the beautiful rose pendent done in diamonds and rubies, which was complemented perfectly by the matching earrings that papa gave her. It was a very aesthetically pleasing design (plan on wearing it myself someday). I missed Sudha aunty who could not make it because somebody had gone in labour. Don't even want to think about mine.

16th August

28th August is the date set for my *SaadhPurai*. My family back home was informed and were expected to arrive on the 27th. The brother is supposed to gift a saree and a few other formalities are observed. About a hundred ladies are invited and a small *pooja* is performed. There was going to be a small ladies *sangeeth* and even dancing. My back pain however was worsening by the day. This is a common symptom, so nothing to be alarmed about. Yesterday was also my first Lamaze class. Should have started it earlier; not only are the classes informative, but are also highly entertaining. Around eleven more expectant mothers joined me and almost all were first time mothers. One of them even looked like she would go into labour anytime. Such a huge stomach! It was surprising to learn that she was carrying a single baby; I was expecting her to be nearing her term with twins. We did a lot of breathing exercises, a few light stretches, learnt how to handle a new born baby and most importantly ensured that Sameer learnt how to change diapers.

29th August

So tired! So very exhausted. The *SaadhPurai* function was a success. The skit which Ravi and Simar had prepared was enjoyed by all. Everybody commented on my small belly and said that I was carrying a boy. Ha! Amusing! Like their eyes could scan through my flesh. Wonder why we even bother going through an ultrasound with such gifted people around. I am curious to know about your gender, though not that it matters. Simple curiosity is all. I had a good mind to ask Dr. Sudha about it but Sameer put his foot down.

"No way! Why do you not want to wait? Please don't spoil the excitement and mystery of the child birth. It is now just a matter of a few more months. Please don't let your curiosity get the better of you".

Well that was the end of the discussion. I am very sure Dr. Sudha wouldn't have obliged me anyway. Getting back to other issues, I have lot of packing to do. We (as in Sameer, Ravi, Simar and me) are leaving for Mysore today for two nights. This is going to be my last holiday for quite some time. *Dada* and *dadi* were pretty apprehensive about sending me but agreed after the three of them had solemnly promised to take utmost care of me. As for me, I was looking forward to having lots of *Mysore masala dosas.*

31st August

All good things must come to an end. I bid sad goodbyes to Ravi and Simar as they flew back yesterday. They are so much fun to be with, and Ravi is an absolute riot. We had a really great time in Mysore. Did a lot of sightseeing. The Mysore palace was magnificent. Roamed around in the Brindavan Gardens, checked out the railway museum and sat by the Karanji lake.

We unfortunately couldn't go to the zoo. It wasn't possible to walk so much and it also made no sense to visit a zoo without you. My brother and sister fussed a lot over me and ensured my comfort. Sameer could not be with us all time as most of it was spent in our Mysore showroom. In unrelated news judging by the amount you kicked in my womb all through the trip, you will be the next Messi!

1st September

Congratulations my child on completing your seven month and starting your eighth. You are growing up just fine going by the latest ultrasound scan and the last visit to the clinic. Slightly on the smaller side (going by the measurement) but nothing to be worried about.

"It is easier to push out a smaller kid as compared to a large one. Don't worry, both you and your baby are doing great".

I had a lot of apprehensions about labour and asked umpteen questions to reassure myself. Let me be honest with you. I am petrified of labour since I dread the pain. Have asked so many mothers about what level of pain I am to expect and the answers have left me more nervous than ever. My threshold of pain tolerance is low (probably non-existent). Dr. Sudha tried to get me to relax. We discussed about pain killers, epidurals and helpful breathing techniques. But I am still so scared. She recommended that I watch a birthing video to prepare myself from the viewpoint of what exactly to expect. Today just to keep myself distracted, taught Sudhir far more than he wanted. It was only when he started his non-stop yawning did I let him go. Must teach him few a manners next time.

15th September

It was my birthday yesterday. My 24th. Got a smart *Versace* watch with a gold dial from Sameer. Had actually been hinting at it from the past fortnight. *Dadi-dada* gave me a *Louis Vuitton* purse. My first LV! Sameer served me breakfast in bed. I simply do not understand why he even attempts to cook? He is clueless as to what ingredients complement each other and has no knowledge about spices. The grilled coleslaw sandwich was very bad and there was no *aloo* in the half burnt and half undone *aloo parathas*. But have to give him full credit for the excellent presentation and earnest effort gone into preparing it. It could have fooled anyone into thinking it was gourmet food.

Went out for lunch with my friends. I missed the last three meets; once when I was in Kolkata, then when I was travelling to Coorg and then during the last one, I was in Mysore. Giving them a treat today at Mainland China. Have been craving Chinese food for some time. The whole gang is here with the exception of Julie (somebody will always be travelling; I do not remember the last time when all eight of us were together). We took a separate room which is always a better option with us ladies talking continuously. Over *cracking spinach, chilly baby corn* and *spicy vegetables* we talked at length about my pregnancy. Finally after ending a meal with *darsaan* (tasty!) we bid adieu to each other. They gifted me a very pretty maternity dress which is a couple sizes too big. No problem!

According to my doctor I still have lot of expanding to do.

Slept the entire evening. Nowadays I tire very easily. *Dadi* and *dada* joined us for dinner. Sameer and I spent the night looking at our photo albums- another one of my favourite hobbies and we updated my pregnancy journal with photographs. God I have started looking huge!

20th September

I have changed your profession. You are no longer a football player; you are now an acrobat. How do I know that you will be one? Simple. Your continuous somersaults inside me! Don't you get tired? You are wearing me out now. Sameer has gone to Delhi for a meeting today. Missing him so much. He has really cut down on his travelling during these past few months, but today's meeting was unavoidable. Anyway he is returning tomorrow evening and in the meantime I can peacefully catch up with all my regular serials. The good part about family soaps is that you can watch them after a gap of months and yet feel that you haven't missed anything. My stomach seems to be expanding by the day and my face feels swollen. Also the number of stretch marks keep increasing despite various (unsuccessful) purported remedies. Fighting a losing battle. I get a couple of suits stitched and they are already undersized in a matter of weeks. I am also losing my sense of visual depth and often end up bumping into objects. Let me tell you about my style of walking. I don't walk, I waddle. Sameer has nick named me 'waddle duck'. Clipping my toe nails has become a lengthy task as I am not able to reach my toes. Walking has also slowed down because of the weight. Turning from one side to the other on the bed is also not easy. They however say that I still have a long way to go!

9th October

The only thing predictable about life is its unpredictability. Day before as I was celebrating the start of my ninth month, just as I was inching closer to holding my baby in my arms, a mother lost her son forever. Sameer's second cousin Alka lost her 18 year old son Aakash in a motorcycle accident.

If the news managed to leave us shell-shocked, then what would be the state of mother who lost her only child? How would she take the news of her child, whom she had nurtured with all her love, being killed in a random moment of callous indifference? She had sheltered him from vices like alcohol, but was unable to protect him from a drunk driver. Her heart would have been crushed after seeing her son's lifeless corpse. He was her pride, her joy and her love. She always dreamt of his future, discussed his studies and spoke of his virtues. He had been a brilliant student, never the one to shun hard work. We all had such high hopes pinned on him.

Since they were based in Kolkata I met them frequently and thought very highly of Aakash. Today all those dreams, ambitions and hopes lie shattered. He's been cruelly punished for no fault of his. Though he never touched alcohol, he had to pay the price of another's addiction to this vice with his own life. My heart went out to Alka *didi* whose anguish couldn't be contained. He had gone in the night to get some medicines for her fever. "I'll be back in a jiffy, mummy. Take care. I love you a lot". These were his last words before he left his mother forever. *Didi* continued to blame herself, as everyone tried to console her by saying that it was God's will.

Are there any words which can console a devastated mother? Life of a child without his mother is said to be tough, but what about the life of a mother without her child? She dies a thousand deaths every day. Relatives were arriving to sympathize. All were offering words of condolence. Your grandparents too left for Kolkata to be with *didi* in her time of grief. No one will ever be able to gauge her feelings, understand her loss, or what she's going through. Life is so unpredictable. Live today as if there is no tomorrow. Gather as much happiness you can today for tomorrow might never come. Little did she know that Aakash would never return from his seemingly innocuous errand. She never even got a chance to say bye. I pray to God to give her strength to face these troubled times.

15th October

Dada and *dadi* are back from Kolkata. I am told not to think about what has happened. I had been pondering over it from quite some time and was even beginning to question the futility of life itself.

"Life is never fair Simran, there are times when you get more than you deserve and there will be moments when you protest at its cruel unfairness. Death is inevitable but that does not mean you stop living. Time is the greatest healer. Even Alka will get on with her life eventually. Life moves on and never stops for anyone. You have a life that is growing inside you and you cannot let your grief for another affect the health of your baby. Now smile and let's start preparations for the arrival of our little angel. I think it is now time for us to prepare the bag you will need in the hospital as you can go into labour anytime."

Why did *dadi* have to talk about labour? It leaves me fearful. I get scared just thinking about it. Sameer is very apprehensive about it too. He decided to watch the birthing video to see if it would be suitable for me. He could not complete it and absolutely forbade me to watch it. What sort of horror was in store for me? If it was too much even for Sameer to see, then how on earth am I supposed to go through with it? I have heard enough of the greatness of a mother who's willing to tolerate unbearable pain just to bring a cherished part of her into this world, but at that moment such noble thoughts were far from my mind. I am already thinking about a C section but nobody else is willing to even consider it.

A few used baby clothes, which *dadi* had procured from some of her friends who had recent child births in their house (because we cannot use any new clothing for the baby till the eighth day) lay by my side. I wondered why this accepted norm was being observed even in such modern times. There are so many traditions which we follow blindly just so as not to invite any misfortune. Tried to convince her about giving a few of these age old traditions a rest. But the words fell on deaf ears.

All the various clothing items were sanitised and washed thoroughly. A baby kit, a small packet of diapers, lots of cloth nappies of various sizes and baby blankets were all arranged in two separate bags. My toiletries and gowns were packed alongside your clothes. Now we were all set. Suresh *bhaiya* was to stay in the house at all times. *Dadi* was firm in staying with me through this.

Please guys give me a break. The due date is still a month away. Also it is becoming very difficult to walk now with all the weight I've gained. Have put on 5 Kgs in the last month alone. My belly seems to precede me by quite a bit. There is a lot of uneasiness everytime I move and if it were not for the fear of pain I would have deliberately bought the birth forward. Go to the hospital, deliver and be done with it.

31st October

This morning there was slight pain in the stomach. Within minutes of mentioning it everyone rushed me to Dr Sudha's clinic. After an internal examination (which was extremely painful and I screamed in agony) it was declared, much to everybody's delight that my cervix had softened and within a day or two you would arrive. Every day the last fortnight I was constantly hounded by everyone about your arrival date. Relatives and friends from all across kept calling up to find out "if anything happened". Sameer would call up every hour from work and enquire if I needed to be rushed to the hospital. I want to tell everybody to back off. Please let the baby decide when it wants arrive. I want to shout it out but obviously don't do so (cannot really be downright rude to anyone except Sameer).

I am as nervous as everybody around me is excited. It was now just a matter of a day or two. If it happens now, then you would be arriving two weeks earlier than your due date but that is alright according to Sudha aunty as latest scan revealed that you have crossed 2.5 Kgs and are ready to make your entry into this world.

1st November

I felt small spasms of pain in the morning and was taken to the hospital. *Dada* went about with the registration formalities and Sameer took me to the birthing suite. It was a beautiful, large room with a huge bed which could be divided into two halves (I would shortly learn why). I was made to change into hospital robes. The pain was now coming at shorter intervals and for a longer duration. These were the wretched contractions which I had been warned about. Dr Sudha attached a lot of tubes from a nearby machine to my stomach.

"This is to monitor the heartbeat of the baby."

God my own heart was pounding in fear and excitement. As the pain started increasing so did the number of nurses. Mummy was waiting outside while Sameer held my hand throughout.

Nothing you hear, or talk about, or see can ever prepare you for the kind of life wrenching pain that is going to be inflicted upon you while you give birth to a child. The pain was tearing my body apart. It was nothing like what I had ever experienced. I screamed, shouted and ranted. Wanted to kick my legs about but they were tied to the bed with firm straps.

"Doctor I am dying. Please do something. I cannot bear it Doctor."

"Mummy help. Sameer please help me."

"Simran please don't shout. Remember what they taught us in the Lamaze class. Take a deep breath through your mouth and slowly breathe out. Then push gen…….."

"Shut up you dog!"

I probably said that a bit too loudly because later *dadi* said that she had heard it crisp and clear

Here I was dying with pain. In the midst of excruciating agony because of these life numbing contractions and my genius husband asks me to breathe slowly. Was he an imbecile? Ask him to go through half of what I went through. Ha! Men don't even have the guts to see it. Otherwise would God have not given them the 'pleasure' of child birth? A husband is good enough to just hold his wife's hand and mutter things so stupid that it would anger her even further. Like mine was doing at the moment.

My throat kept drying and small sips of water were offered in between my screams. I will not describe all the gory details. You probably will not want to know about it either. Don't blame you. It would be enough to freak anybody out. The water broke and with a couple of pushes amidst indescribable pain, you emerged. Loud wails filled the room as all my agony magically vanished upon hearing you cry. I lay exhausted while Sameer let go of my hand to hold you. Time seemed to come to a standstill. Tears of joy rolled down Sameer's eyes as he held you while Dr Sudha congratulated me.

"It's a lovely baby boy."

2nd November

My Son! My child! My baby! Thank you for completing my world. Holding you in my arms for the first time was the most beautiful moment of my life. I was ecstatic when I saw my bundle of joy. With your first cries, the most painful period of my life changed into the most blissful one. I cannot pen down all the wonderful feelings I am going through. If only words existed that could express all that I felt. I had read somewhere that having a child is like watching your heart walk out of your body forever. I can now understand the meaning behind it. Today with your birth my heart has decided to no longer be a part of me but has forever taken shape as you.

You are a healthy baby though on the smaller side. Your birth weight was 2.6 Kg. I guess none of my weight gain really passed on to you. You seem so fragile and delicate till you start wailing. You cry for everything. When you're wet or hungry or need to be cleaned. It is your way of communicating your needs to me. I could continue to stare for hours at your sweet face and not be tired. You lay tightly wrapped up in your blanket in your cot. Visitors keep pouring in and it is now that I realize that we have so many friends and relatives in Bangalore. Almost everyone says that you look just like me. Sameer tries to look offended but he too feels that you look perfect as you are. Your grandparents are thrilled to bits. Both your *dada* and *nana* called up everyone to inform them about the arrival of their grandson and your *dadi* and *nani* are preparing to start shopping for their angel. Seriously how many things can a tiny baby need?

Sameer has not left my side (or should I say your side) at all. And wonders of wonder, he only takes congratulatory calls. "Simran you have given me all that I could ever ask for." Yes these lovely words would have felt like music to my ears if only he would have been looking towards me while saying them. You see he has eyes only for you. The nurses teach me the correct position to feed you, how to give you a bath and how to wrap you up, but I don't really need any guidance. Once you become a mother you automatically know what's best for your baby. The stitches hurt and I am not allowed to sit for long. But now I cannot complain of any pain. It seems to be too trivial compared to my joy, to deserve a mention.

4th November

You have arrived home today! The whole bungalow has been decorated with blue and white balloons and ribbons. We performed a small prayer in the puja room before proceeding to our room. Now a 40 day confinement period begins. I do not know about other communities but in *Marwari* families, a 40 day period of seclusion needs to be observed after childbirth. This is known as *Jaapa*. Your husband has to shift to another room (I am really going to miss Sameer, though he has promised not to follow this particular tradition too strictly) and during this time you have to lead a pretty dreadful life. All food is excessively full of ghee. We believe in the goodness of ghee. Nothing benefits the baby and mother as much as it does. So everything that is served to you is either cooked in or served with unheard quantities of *ghee*. No spices, nothing tangy, just plain boiled vegetables, lots of milk (4 glasses a day), almonds, and *ghee*.

I am already bored of this diet. How am I to survive another 5 weeks? And you cannot read, watch TV or write (I write a few lines when no one is watching) and you are not supposed to talk much (I make up for that by singing to you all the time). Kajal *maasi* (your chaperone who has arrived from Kolkata yesterday) fortunately knows her work and looks after us just fine. I hope together we manage to bide away this time where all I have to look forward to is eating and sleeping.

Also there is the rather pressing matter of naming you. The actual ceremony will be held on 13th December and Sameer and *dada* are scouting for a suitable venue. However the question which arises now is to do with who should get the honour of naming you. I sort of want *Shreyanz* while Sameer is keen on *Samarth*. Our arguments over this get louder by the day. Honestly speaking, I don't even know why I am fighting over this, when I am not so particular about *Shreyanz*. I really want to think it over. You will have to live with your name for the rest of your life and since you do not have any say in it, I should think up of a very good one on your behalf.

9th November

Having too many sleepless nights. You love to sleep during the day and stay up in the nights. Why sweetie, why? I spoke to your pediatrician Dr Bhatt (recommended highly by Dr Sudha) who has given me a few tips on how to change your circadian rhythm before you make it permanent. During the day I must keep the room brightly lit and during the night, it is to be kept dark even if you are up. Also I must wrap you up tightly in the night as this will help you sleep better. I am trying out these suggestions and hopefully you will develop a proper sleeping pattern. I don't want to appear like a nag who is constantly complaining about her child but there is also the problem of feeding you. You want to be fed every hour in contrast to the three hour gap recommended by the doctor. I try to sing you a lullaby, but to no avail. You don't stop howling till you are fed. This is also causing a sore back to add to my misery.

I still can't decide on your name; I so wish you were able to talk and tell me what you would like to be called.

14th November

Happy children's day! This is your first one and you have been gifted clothes, rattles, a pram and blankets. Everybody around is going crazy with buying you gifts. They just need an excuse. I had previously talked about how much a baby could need. You sure need a lot of things alright. Clothes, nappies (lots and lots of them) blankets and your own toilette cupboard (there are so many kinds of oils-massage oil, baby oil, hair oil and creams- a separate one for your face, one for the body and the most importantly a nappy rash cream). But others seem more frivolous.

I already have enough for three kids and this is.......just the start. Where do I keep it? You have around 8 pairs of shoes even though you haven't yet started walking! Seriously, what a waste.

You are an intelligent child; I can already see signs of it. You have managed to stay one step ahead of me all this while. Dr Bhatt's tips don't work with you. You still enjoy your sleep during the days while the nights witness colorful histrionics which just keep getting louder and every light in the house comes on. I am not exaggerating, but I am already getting dark circles. In other related news the food is now getting on to me.

I hate it.

H A T E I T.

I want to throw up all the ghee. Not to mention the weight that I have put on. *Dadi* has removed the weighting scale from the bathroom and hidden it someplace where I can't find it, but the full length mirror in the bathroom tells me loudly and clearly about all excess adipose that I've gained in the interim.

20th November

Your first vaccination! This was also the first time I headed out since your birth. Because you are exclusively on my feed I have to tag along. At least I got to step out of the room. Phew, it had started to get real claustrophobic in there. It was time for your vaccination. Not a very pleasant thought for either or us. The DPT vaccination causes high fever accompanied by a lot of pain, but it's an essential health requirement. You were very brave throughout except for the time when the needle was jabbed into your thigh. You made your disapproval loud and clear by wailing endlessly.

Your growth is progressing well and you have now crossed the 3 Kg mark. Dr Bhatt was very happy with your growth. I have been asked to continue with breast feeding.

There might be a solution in sight regarding your name: *Dada* suggested 'Vatsal' (joy).

V-A-T-S-A-L. *VATSAL*.

The name has a very nice ring to it. I keep saying it in different ways and it is starting to sound even better.

Sameer took immediate liking to it. You have bought immense joy to our lives and the name thus seems apt. I mulled over it while I spent yet another sleepless night next to you. Sameer has offered to watch over you in his room so that I can snatch a couple of hours of undisturbed sleep but the thought of you being away is less appetizing than it sounds.

3rd December

It is done. You are now officially Vatsal Jain!

Dadi wasn't very convinced but everyone else unanimously agreed that it was a good choice. Everybody is now getting busy with the preparations for the ceremony on the 13th. The cards were sent out and calls made to relatives near and far. Arrangements for their stay and travel are being taken care of. The function is going to be held in one of the best five star hotels in the city. What can be better than such a grand setting for our prince? Pushpa *Bhua* will be arriving in a couple of days to help *dadi*. Almost all the other relatives will be here by the 10th, including *nana*, *nani*, *mama* and *maasi*. They have not yet seen you and can barely wait.

17th December

Vatsal you had a very grand naming function. Your dad went all out to give you a fantastic welcome. The function was an extravaganza which is going to be remembered by everybody for a long time. The theme of the occasion was *Krishna Kanhaiya.* The banquet hall looked like a scene right out of *Brindavan.* Huts of different sizes were setup randomly, all over. Laser Lighting and graphical projections were used to create the illusion of a river flowing by. An arc of peacock feathers was placed at the entrance and numerous sweets and dry fruits were hung in earthen pots. Large cutouts of scenes from *Krishna's* life adorned the walls. Fans made of peacock feathers were handed out to guests as they arrived and they left with small silver flutes (a gift from *nana*) on the way out.

Inside those randomly placed huts, there was a *mehandiwali*, a fortune teller, a bangle maker and a puppet dance show. The food looked delicious! I said "looked" because I wasn't allowed to taste it. I need to watch my diet because of your colic. The meals that I was forced to partake in was bland beyond belief.

Sameer looked dashing in his bandh gala but alas, the same couldn't be said of me. The designer ghagra and the beautiful jewelry could not conceal the layers of fat which now adorned me like acne. I was huge. I had crossed the upper limit of fat and now resembled a water melon. That did it; I am not going to have any more ghee. Time to put my foot down once and for all. With all this fat, I looked like I had aged beyond my years. Very soon I might end up looking like Sameer's mom instead of yours. I so hate this *Jaapa* system.

Most our relations from your dad's side were there along with quite a few from mine. Many cousins who had travelled from

Kolkata were taken aback at how fat I had become. *Nana* and *nani* had bought tons of gifts for everyone. It is customary for the maternal side to give gifts when their daughter has a child. You have received 51 sets of clothes, 11 blankets, 21 pairs of shoes, 31 toys, a pram, lots of hats and caps and many other knick-knacks. And these were only from your *nana.* Many more gifts from others quickly piled up and I am clueless as to where to keep all of it. How on earth would you ever be able to use even a fraction of it? I think I will donate most of it as I have no way of using so many of them. We were both exhausted before the day ended. Feeding you was one hell of a task in that heavy ghagra. I left a little early with you and Simar accompanied us. I just wanted to lie down…..

Today Sameer is shifting back to our room. He is very excited but I know his bubble is about to burst. His sleepless nights will now begin.

25th December

Merry Christmas Vatsal! Today our last guest, Pushpa *Bhua* left. She had made my life difficult again. No talking, no shouting (now just whom was I going to shout at), no TV, continue with eating this and that and her zillion restrictions.

This time though I didn't really mind it so much because I know her intentions are good. I do not want to be ashamed like the last time around, but nonetheless I relaxed a bit more with her gone.

Kajal *maasi*, your nanny is a big help. She takes good care of you and your things. I have now started massaging you but it is not a very pleasurable task because you keep crying. Another thing, each time you cry for more than a few seconds at a stretch, everybody in the house including Radha *maasi* will ask me that most dreaded of questions first time mothers despise.

"Why are you making Vatsal *baba* cry?"

Sarcasm* Because I LOVE to make you cry. I makes me feel GREAT! *sarcasm.

Really now, come people, this is how babies communicate, but that's apparently too much to understand. I can already foresee you being pampered and spoilt by everyone around. You are like a fancy new toy, all the adults become children again when you are around, passing you from one set of adoring arms to another (but always under the ever watchful eyes of Kajal). Before I forget to mention, you and I are leaving for Kolkata on the 10th January for almost a month.

Yay! Also Santa left you a small swing (which you will be able to use after a few months. Santa must have thought that it perfectly complements your cuteness). He hopes that this bribe will help you change your sleeping habits to fit a saner schedule.

1st January 2004

HAPPY NEW YEAR SWEETHEART! We rang in the New Year with a quiet dinner in my room. I decorated it with a few heart shaped red balloons with a few aromatic candles lending a soft touch which was further accentuated by light romantic music playing in the background. Our meal consisted of *roti, black daal* and *paneer ki subzi* (this is all that *dadi* agreed to let me have and that too after being assured of the pedigree of the restaurant from where I had ordered it).

Finally had some alone time with Sameer. We fed each other while whispering sweet nothings, and for this, we have you to thank (you decided to let us enjoy the moment for a change and slept on time, if only you could make this a daily habit). I don't want to sound like a constant drip but the last few weeks have been hard on us as we rarely got to spend time with each other. We were together in flesh but not in spirit. All we did, spoke and thought, centered around you.

All the sweet nothings, the endless chitter-chatter, the messages and the romantic moments, all seem like a thing of the past. I have been warned that it is bound to happen; as we tend to get busy with the newest addition to the family, spousal neglect sort of happens. Nevertheless yesterday was great and hope this year will bring much more happiness in our lives.

9th January

I am going to have to pay a lot of money for excess baggage. The suitcases are piling on mainly because of your needs. There are so many things to take along. Your pram, the bottle sterilization kit, your countless cloth nappies (I don't like the idea of you being in diapers), the thick blankets, your baby mattress, let's not even get into your clothes and accessories. As for me, one medium sized suitcase was enough. There are not too many clothes which will fit my gigantic frame.

How I regret listening to your *dadi* vis-à-vis a ghee rich diet. Sameer called me his sweet pumpkin in jest, but it is true I do look like one. My eyes actually appear smaller because they are sort of hidden behind my bulging cheeks. My long forgotten curves have transformed into a shapeless blob. I now need to get my suits tailored because I can't even fit into XL sizes available in most shops. Why, just the other day we had gone shopping and the salesperson (who I swear was older to me) actually addressed me as AUNTY!!!!! Your dad nearly died laughing. That harmless salutation was a real wake up call. From the day I land in Kolkata (well, make it the next day) I have decided to start working out and return to my original self. Kajal *Maasi* has already left by train and will reach there tomorrow. This is going to be your first flight and I think I will save your boarding pass and ticket. Please be on your best behavior tomorrow. To tell you the truth even I am very nervous about flying alone with you. I will be following the doctor's instructions to the word. Two drops of otogesic in each ear and you are to be fed during takeoff and landing.

Looking forward to going there, but Sameer is understandably upset. This is the first time you are going away and he is going to miss you so much. I consoled him by telling him to look forward to a month of peaceful sleep.

11th January

You can never truly predict how a day might turn out. Yesterday was one of the most memorable days of my life. I had never been so surprised. It was an early morning flight and we were both still quite groggy when I bid bye to both *dadi* and *dada* who were a little upset that we were leaving. You started howling when we reached the airport. Sameer requested the airport security permission to help me out and his request was granted. Sameer got us the boarding passes while I tried to pacify you. Thank God for Sameer helping me out with all the baggage. Try as much as I did, I could not pack light. The airline very gracefully allowed us to carry excess baggage without charging us for it. However the cabin baggage was bulky and I had no option but to take along with me.

They actually allowed Sameer to get through the security just so he could help us!

Wait something wasn't adding up here.

God I've been rather silly! "Sameer are you travelling with

us?" I asked rather anxiously. He just smiled.

"God please tell me. Are you? Is that why they allowed you in?"

"Are you not smart or what?"

"No riddles. Are you flying with me or going elsewhere? (I was hoping that he was coming along with me and wasn't on one of his single day business trips)

He picked up a newspaper and pretended to read it.

This was too much to bear and I pulled his boarding pass from his pocket. It read "KF 623 flying to Kolkata".

"Yaaaaaaaaaaaaay!" I shouted and hugged him hard.

Everyone stared at me (some even a little fearfully like as if I was terrorist).

Sameer was embarrassed and turned beet red after my overt show of emotions. He had never been comfortable about public displays of affection.

But I was too thrilled to care. "My husband is coming along to my dad's place and it is a wonderful surprise for me." I said to a lady nearby.

"Oh that is so sweet. I wish my husband would do something like that for me". She nudged her husband. He ignored her completely.

How could I not stop smiling? This was one of the most beautiful surprises that he has ever given me. No wonder we had been allowed so much more baggage. How could I not realize it earlier?

Sameer was amused by my reaction. "So I can still manage to surprise you sweetheart."

I hugged him and did not let go even though he kept protesting.

I love him so much.

15th January

The past five days have just flown by and all I have done is tell everyone about Sameer's delightful gesture. It got to a stage where I was told not to bring up this subject again.

He is flying back tomorrow. We had a great time together. I initially thought of returning with him (I wanted to surprise him too) but then thought better of it as I didn't really want to cut short my vacation. I think I'll surprise him by leaving a little earlier than planned. That should do the trick.

How on earth can I hope to lose weight when I am in Kolkata? The tempting food and ultra-delicious sweets would just not let me stick to my resolution. So rather than torture myself with false promises for an entire month, I decided to forego my weight loss resolution. Besides all my well-meaning aunts assured me that I would be back to normal within a few months. Breast feeding, they told me, helps a lot in weight reduction.

I must confess that I don't get to see much of you. My family has divided the day into various slots and everyone has a fixed schedule of spending time with you. I only get to be with you whenever you are hungry, so I've been killing time by reading and watching movies I've missed during the last three months.

The day after, we are going to see a potential groom for Simar *maasi*. *Nana* and *Nani* have approved of him and his family. He's name is Aakash and he's from Delhi (looks cute in the snaps). Simar is nervous and excited. She met his parents last week and found them lovely. So let's keep our fingers crossed for good news in the coming days.

18th January

Aakash is so, so, so, cute. Totally *chocolaty* looks. Nice features, very fair, good physique (works out every day for two hours) a slight accent (has completed his post-graduation in America) and a dimpled smile. Height would be the only drawback which prevented him from being considered a model. He is just 5' 7". Spoke at length to him and was very happy with what I heard, gave Simar the go ahead from my side. He was very charming and I instantly approved of him the minute he said that you are the cutest baby he has ever seen.

Yes flattery does get many things done son. Getting back to the matchmaking, though both your *maasi* and Aakash like each other, they want to meet a couple of times more before taking the 'Big' decision. Obviously we will be accompanying them. You remember I told you that the potential partners are always with a brother or sister? I am keeping your dad abreast of all the current developments. He will drop in if they happen to finally agree.

24th January

Congratulations!

You now have a "Mausa". Yesterday we got to know about him consenting and then we had a family discussion (your dad was with us most of the time on phone) and then a very nervous Simar finally said yes too!

"What's taking you so long dude?" questioned Ravi.

He was almost perfect. But I knew exactly how she was feeling at this moment. Three years ago, I was in the same situation and felt so confused. Yes, everything might look perfect but a girl still feels unsure about the future, nervous about becoming a part of an unknown family while adjusting to an alien environment. This one decision determines how the rest of your life unfolds. Arranged marriage is nothing short of a gamble. I know the spiel of slowly discovering and knowing your spouse et al, but it is still very disconcerting if you ask me.

I mean how much can you know about a person in just a few meetings (during which they obviously would be on their best behavior)? However elders argue that arranged marriages are more stable and successful than love marriages. I personally think a love cum arranged marriage is the best option, bringing to the relationship, the best of both worlds.

They make such a good looking couple. Sameer came by the morning flight and we decided to go out for breakfast.

"He is very good looking but not more than me" was you self -obsessed dad's first quip (and your *dadi* is solely to be blamed for it, always brainwashing him into believing that he is so very dashing).

"Ha! Ha! Mr. Sameer Jain he is far cuter."

"Ravi what do you think? Which of your brother- in-laws is better looking?" Your dad tried to put Ravi *mama* in a tight spot.

"Both are hunks but it is my nephew Vatsal who is the most handsome of all." Said your very clever uncle, and who was going to argue with that!

Aakash bonded very well with not only us but our cousins too. The whole razzmatazz was present in the morning for breakfast. We actually made so much noise that the manager had to request us to keep our voices down for the benefit of the other diners.

Aakash's younger brother Vishal (God knows why is he named so , when he is even shorter than his brother) initially felt out of place but soon joined in our merry making.

Today evening is the *dastoor* for which dad has booked the

ball room of another fancy five star hotel in Kolkata. Everyone is expected to be there. Today is also going to be the first time where you are presented to all our relatives since a lot of them are yet to see you.

25th January

Growing tired of the congratulatory calls we have had to receive. The phone keeps ringing r-e-l-e-n-t-l-e-s-s-l-y. The function was a success yesterday. There were around 160 guests. Lots of envelopes were handed to you with so many "very cute" compliments (let's not get into the "My God! How huge you have become" comments which were aimed at me).

Simar and Aakash looked very stunning, though I (along with many relatives) noticed that even in flats she appeared slightly taller than Aakash. When a couple of aunts mentioned this, Ravi was quick to reply that "good things come in small packages." Aakash is heading back to Delhi tomorrow along with his family and will be spending the day with Simar. For once no escorts are required, though Ravi did ask me to tag along, but Sameer put his foot down and asked him to take it easy. *Nana* and Aakash's dad are going to decide today on the wedding date and venue. Wow, lots of merriment on the way!

28th January

Sameer left for Bangalore yesterday. Missing him already. Aakash left the day before. Finally things appear to be settling down. The date for the wedding is set for 12th December and it will be held in Kolkata. Aakash will arrive with his Baraat here.

So much work needs to be done and so many preparations

need to be seen to. Ravi and *nana* are planning and discussing arrangements. I too chip in with the occasional suggestion. They are going to select a hotel this week for the *baraat*. *Nani* and my *bhua* are busy finalizing jewelry designs. Simar *maasi* is always busy on the phone talking either to Aakash or to his family members.

However, apart from a suggestion or two, I have nothing much to do. We are leaving for Bangalore on the 4th because it's your dad's birthday on the 5th, and I have a wonderful gift for him. It is a beautiful gold and diamond Rolex watch which he had been eyeing for some time. I had placed an order a month back and your *dadi* informed me about its arrival yesterday. This gift will more than make up for me not getting him anything for our anniversary. Touch wood, you have been an angel during this visit. You have not troubled me; you've started waking up less during the nights and you haven't had any health issues either. Very soon you will be three months old. You seem to be putting on weight and look quite chubby (actually chubby is what everybody now calls me now, boo hoo!).

3rd February

Will leave tomorrow. *Nani* and *maasi* get all teary at the mention of it. They just don't want to let go of you. I am upset at leaving too, but know we will meet again shortly for the engagement in Delhi which also happens to be Aakash's birthday.

You have been pampered crazy, but thankfully you are too young to be spoilt. It has been a terrific holiday. *Nana- nani* have welcomed two new members in their family, Aakash and you. Met my friends yesterday and proudly showed paraded you like a prized trophy. Raksha's got engaged and will be leaving for the States to settle down there. Tanisha has opened her own boutique and though I promised her that I will be visiting her store I don't think I will be able to make it.

Helped *nani* decide what gifts should be given to all of Aakash's and our relatives on the occasion of Simar's marriage.

A wedding in our community means endless rituals, umpteen gifts and never ending expenses. Thank God, *nana* is well-off and can afford to realize his daughter's dream wedding, but why am I boring you with all these details? You will very soon be on your way home. Everybody has missed you terribly and anxiously await your arrival.

6th February

Sameer had a good birthday. His favorite breakfast, a nice movie and an Italian lunch and dinner with family and friends, which was rounded off with the icing to the cake, our gift. Quite literally.

I had the Rolex gift case concealed inside a cake box and then layered it with cake and lots of icing. He cut into the cake and was surprised when the knife hit something solid.

"Did you happen to make this cake Simi? It is too hard to cut through." He joked (well for the sake of his own health I hope he was joking! My cakes are not all that bad). When he removed the icing and saw the box he understood that it was just a sham cake. He loved our gift. I got a hug (we were amongst relatives remember so all I can get is just that) while you got lots of kisses.

We celebrated your dad's birthday and now have to plan for your *dada*'s which is on the 10th of this month. We have decided to send them for a couple of days to Angsana Spa and Resort which has opened up near Bangalore. *Dada* appears tired and a few days of relaxation will do him good.

8th March

A cute hamper arrived for you yesterday from Aakash uncle. An assortment of clothes, toys and chocolates (I guess they were for me because you are too young for chocolates) in a nice baby bag. After thanking him on your behalf, I reciprocated his gesture with some nice gifts. Sameer is very busy with yet another showroom launch. Goes early, comes home late and is always on his phone. So we are not nearly getting enough time to spend together.

I sort of complained (just happened to mention it a few times) about it to him and pat came the very terse reply, "Oh you have noticed! Nowadays you are the one who has no time for me. Right now I am busy with work but what about all these past months? We have hardly even been talking. I know Vatsal is the new entrant in our lives, But Simi he is supposed to bring us closer. Every moment of your time is just meant for him now. Am I still a part of your life? An honest answer please. I want the three of us to be a family and not be alienated from one another."

OUCH, that hurt.

My initial reaction was of anger. How dare he conveniently put all the blame on me? But upon deeper pondering and self-introspection I realized that he was right. I was so involved with you that I have been ignoring Sameer totally. Previously I would wake him up in the morning, have a chat while he read the paper with his morning tea, have breakfast together, arrange the clothes he would wear to work, look forward to him coming home, go out for long drives and talk endlessly about nothing in particular till he fell asleep. Now all my attention has been focused on you and I have been unconsciously ignoring him. The only thing we talk about is you. Nothing wrong with that, except that he deserves some more time and attention. Need to plan something special for him.

12th March

It's been a 'make Sameer feel special' week all right. Dropping notes for him to read everywhere (on his pillow, mirror, car, lunch box, inside his newspaper and even in his wallet). There is now a flower (taken from our garden) on his tea tray. Lot of sweet SMSs have been sent to his cell phone.

After you sleep, I make it a point to spend some time with him. He is obviously enjoying all the attention being showered upon him, except for the one time when I had a bouquet delivered to him in the middle of a very heated meeting with his staff. Lesson learnt- no more bouquets, but it is becoming tiresome. Looking after you, the house, Sameer, unwanted relatives and of course the cooking (Radha *maasi* has gone on her annual leave for one month which will definitely extend into two).

I don't have any time for myself anymore. Instead of Batman, Superman and Spiderman, they should have comic strips on the super woman modeled on the, wait for it, THE LADY OF THE HOUSE! We ladies always have so much to juggle, but what hurts, is the fact that we aren't appreciated enough for these efforts. We come from a country which worships female deities but treats regular women very casually. We don't mind doing any and everything for our families but please, at least learn to appreciate it or say thank you. Take heed of this and always treat the ladies in your life with almost respect and appreciation (especially your mother).

I am yet to start devoting time to myself. Need to start working out soon and lose all the unwanted fat (have actually started looking like a behenji).

20th March

Felt like a heroine from the Bollywood movies. The sky opened up in the evening. Sameer arrived early from work today and *dada-dadi* were out for a house warming ceremony.

I remembered that your clothes were still drying on the terrace and ran up to fetch them. It took me two trips to get most of it to dry safety. On the third trip, I heard *have you ever really loved a woman* playing in the background. I turned around slowly................and saw Sameer standing on the terrace with his arms outstretched in the rain.

I did not need any further invitation and *raaaaaaan* to join him.

Together we danced with gay abandon to all of *Bryan Adams* most memorable songs!

It was a very surreal moment. The rain, the music and just the two of us. The smell of the petrichor enveloped us.

We weren't bothered about the rain pouring down heavily. We had eyes only for each other. A beautiful evening which I will remember and cherish forever.

30th March

Each time I plan to start my workout something has to happen. You were down with a viral fever for a week! I hope it had nothing to do with me dancing for hours in the rain a few days earlier. It was a tough week. Found it very difficult to see you crying all the time. You had a high fever with a stomach infection. Had planned on starting baby feed for you but had to put it off for the next month.

Dr Bhatt kept emphasizing on the importance of mother's milk especially when the child was unwell. Both you and I spent sleepless nights. There wasn't much help on the home-front as *dadi* and *dada* along with Sameer had left for Rajesh mama and Tara mami's daughter's wedding. I had to skip it to look after you. Sameer would not hear of me travelling with you being ill. To make matters worse Kajal *maasi* too was down with a throat infection and I could not let her near my precious darling for the fear of her infecting you, so all in all, a very tough fortnight. It has left me with a very bad backache.

It is only when we become parents that we realize how much our parents have done for us. Their sacrifices, their sleepless nights, always putting our wishes before their own, their care and concern for us can never be repaid or matched. Seriously only now can I now truly appreciate my parents. Previously we would assume that it is their duty to provide for us, but experience has taught me that it went above and beyond such mundane notions.

I now make it a point to keep thanking my parents for all that they have done and are continuing to do for me. Seeing you cry bought tears to my eyes. Now that you are in good health once again your smile makes me so glad.

14th April

Julie, my friend, has finally got engaged. We met along with other friends for lunch today. I got as much attention as Julie herself. Everyone congratulated her and then commented on my girth. GRRR!

It was so irritating. Why can't I stick to my resolution of saying no to fatty foods and yes to exercise? This is becoming embarrassing, we were all halfway through lunch (and I must confess I didn't eat too much for fear of inviting more ridicule) when her fiancée made an appearance. I was quite shocked at his appearance. Though only four years apart, he looked far older than Julie because of his receding hairline and could have passed off as her father. Sneha though informed me that he was Mr. Moneybags himself. He graciously picked up the check despite our protests. The less said about his looks the better. Kept wondering what made her agree to the match. Each to her own I suppose. I have made a few resolutions for myself to observe. They are as follows.

1. No sweets, deserts, chocolates or ice-creams.
2. No pizzas and pastas.
3. No fried calorie rich food.
4. Walk five times a week.
5. Go to the gym thrice a week.
6. To continue with these practices until my weight returned to a more respectable 54 Kgs again.
7. And no shopping till I succeeded (if this wouldn't motivate me then nothing would).

5th May

I have lost 4 kgs already! Not that it is showing however. What difference will removing a drop make to an ocean? That was wise Mr. Sameer's unwanted observation. I am sticking to all my resolutions, though I have to admit that it is making me very cranky.

My uber healthy diet consists of lot of fruits, salads and a wide variety of vegetable juices. The weighing scale is my current best friend. My day starts and ends with me stepping on the scale and religiously jotting down my opening and closing weight.

Though I've lost weight, I still have a long way to go. But this is a step in the right direction. Sameer too has started accompanying me in my morning walks in our neighborhood park and we are getting to spend more time together.

Started with top feed for you last week. We gave you a small spoon of apple puree. You seemed to enjoy it. Now we feed you a small bowl of it, which doubles up as a meal for you. It initially did feel a little strange that you were no longer dependent on me for food, but I am more used to it now. In fact I like it, as it allows me more freedom to move around without having to worry about feeding you endlessly.

You are now able to sit. We help you into a sitting position and you manage to sit for a few minutes before toppling over. All your motor skills match your growth and age and Dr Bhatt is very happy with your progress.

You are one CUTE kid. Every mother thinks of her kid as the cutest but in your case the admiration is far more objective, with everyone who meets you finding you adorable. You have curly dark brown hair, lovely features with a very fair complexion (just like Sameer's), and a sweet smile with two deep dimples (like Ravi *mama*). At birth you looked so much like me but as you grow, the resemblance to Sameer is becoming stronger. I miss those days when everyone kept saying that you looked just like me. Now when they tell that to Sameer, his chest swells with pride and the smile broadens into a grin.

You share a lovely bond with your dad. Your face lights up when he arrives home. You enjoy the way he twirls you and laugh and gurgle wherever you both play *peek-a-boo*. The Sunday massages are done by your dad and I am not allowed to be in the room lest you ask for me. He takes you for strolls in the park, but you always refuse to sit in the pram and keep howling till he picks you up in his arms. Your dad actually likes the fact that you want him more than the pram. Like there is competition.

20th May

You have started teething and all the dreaded symptoms are showing. You put anything that you can get your hands on (and I mean absolutely anything) straight into your mouth. The outcome is a very predictable diarrhea.

You are perpetually cranky, irritated and crying. No toys old or new are able to pacify you. The room is littered with balls of different shapes and sizes, a rocking horse, a swing, building blocks, the musical play gym and teeters, but you are most content only when the television is switched on. What is it about the idiot box and the children? They officially self -appoint the TV as their nanny. If not that, then you just want to be rocked (not in the swing, but in my arms) and I can tell you that they are absolutely sore from having to carry you around all the time. *Dadi* tries to help me and takes you around the garden but to no avail. You just want mummy.

You have a developed a rash round your buttocks and I have to take you to Dr Bhatt before the condition worsens.

25th May

You are down with fever yet again. *Dadi* tries to calm me, by telling me that this is normal when children are teething but it does little to comfort me.

You have lost a lot of weight because of your diarrhea which has been happening for quite some time and now we have to deal with this fever too. You look so frail that you have me worried. All your chubbiness seems to have melted away and to make matters worse you also have a nasal congestion. I am at my wits end. None of the medicines seem to be of any help. The room resembles a pharmacy right now. There are so many bottles of medicine; for fever, for vomiting, for diarrhea, for your cold and even something for your ears. Additionally there is also a plethora of household remedies which *dadi* recommended. *Dada* has asked me to switch doctors but Sameer refuses to do so.

Simar *maasi*'s engagement in Delhi is coming up and instead of helping mom and dad with the preparations, I haven't even started packing yet. Feeling very guilty but cannot shift my focus from you at all. Please get well soon love. Please. Mummy is now in tears.

6th June

The engagement ceremony was a big success. All the big names from our circle of acquaintances were there. A grand function was held in the banquet hall of a leading five star hotel. The *Prince Dance Group* was called to perform and later they led both Simar and Aakash to their seats. Amidst a lot of cheering, they exchanged rings.

I was told that this is what happened. I wasn't really a part of all this though as most of the evening was spent in the hotel room with you. You were down with high fever and wouldn't be pacified by anyone else. Not even *dada* and *dadi*. I made a fleeting appearance at the event. You howled during the two hour flight to and fro and the short the trip was an absolute nightmare. Today, finally the fever has lessened and the temperature hasn't shown any significant increase, so hopefully in a couple of days you will be alright again, but the road to recovery is going to be a very long one. You have lost a lot of weight and have become very weak.

I would have loved to tell you about everyone's outfits but being a boy I am sure you wouldn't be interested. However, let me tell you something. Quite a few people commented on my slimmer figure. I know there is still a long way to go, but it did feel good.

20th June

You crawled! From one end of the room to almost the other end. Such an awesome feeling. It was so exciting that I forgot to capture it on camera. Such a cute sight, too bad I didn't record it for Sameer, but I did call him up and I am sure he was equally excited (or at least he pretended to be) though he was in the middle of an important meeting (him and his never ending meetings). Vatsal I am so proud of you.

And today is a day of double celebrations. Radha *maasi* has also returned. I can now breathe a sigh of relief. Finally I can quit cooking and relax. I had been very upset this past month with your ill health, but as Dr Bhatt told me, kids keep falling ill but also recover quickly. This is how they grow up. Finally no more medicines. I feel so relieved!

5th August

Dada and *dadi* are leaving tonight for Canada. It is a fifteen day holiday which includes seven days on an Alaskan cruise (wish I too could be a part of this trip).

It is *Dadi*'s 50th birthday soon and I organized this to celebrate the occasion in style. I have planned a couple of events during this period. I've decided to invite my friends over on one day and Sameer's on another. It also happens to be a sale period! Most of the malls have their off season sale going on and I intend to make the most of it.

Have lost a little more weight and need new clothes to reflect the fact. I don't fit in my clothes which I had from before you were born or after. So I genuinely need retail therapy.

"Don't go overboard, because you will shed more weight

and then these clothes will become redundant too", advised Sameer.

Now was that a subtle hint that I should lose a little more flab? It wasn't very subtle.

Anyway who cares? Julie and I plan to go berserk. She too needs to pick up her trousseau for her wedding which is coming up in a few months. I really don't need an excuse to shop.

20th August

Rachna's mother passed away because of a massive heart attack. She was also Pinky and Raina's aunt. All three have left for Guwahati for the cremation and last rites. I have met aunty a few times. She was so full of life, always looking at the brighter side and laughing the loudest at the silliest of jokes. Hard to believe she passed away. Why is it so hard to come to terms with death when it is the only inevitable thing which is confirmed at birth? We know we can't run or hide from it but we are still unable to cope with it. I don't think I will be able to handle the death of a loved one. Sameer always says that time will heal everything and life will move on. But does it heal wounds or just give you the strength to carry on with life? I have always been scared of death. Have always feared dying or death taking someone close to me beyond my reach. Death has always been a big mystery for me. A truth of life which I could not come to terms with. Missing your *dadi*, always want her around to help me handle such situations. Thank goodness she is on her way back today.

2nd September

A bad movie can give you a never ending headache. Come to think of it I was the one guilty here, forcing Sameer to watch it too. Had to take a Disprin to rid myself of it. I needn't have bothered with it however, since just seeing you laugh and smile would have been enough to cure me. You have started saying absolute GIBBERISH in a sing song manner. People say that a mother can make out what her kid is saying, but that thus far, I am quite clueless. I think you're attempting to sing the rhymes I play in the room all the time!

You now are able stand (with support). It is hard to keep up with your crawling. I pretend to hide behind a door (always remaining visible to you) and you come crawling straight to me with a triumphant grin on your face. When Sameer tries to play *peek-a-boo* with you, you still come looking for me and he keeps shouting that it is him you are supposed to look for. I always tease him when you do that. I am trying to make you say 'mamma' while Sameer makes you focus on 'papa'. Waiting for your first word. I want to hear you say 'ma' on my birthday. This would be the most cherished gift ever.

10th September

Feeding you is becoming very difficult. You refuse to eat anything which is given to you and want to eat everything that is not offered to you. We take turns to run all over the house to feed you (which is not an easy task as it's a huge house). Sometimes we even have to go outside the house and more often than not to Sharma uncle's place whose large Labrador keeps you distracted while you are being fed. Though he is very nice about it, it still becomes awkward going to his place with a bowl of food in hand and a sheepish grin.

Nani told me that I too was very finicky with my meals and it seems you take after me in this matter. Dr. Bhatt repeatedly has asked me not to fuss over your food and to feed you over long intervals, but I don't pay any heed to that advice, resulting in a perpetual game of tag. This is a common topic of conversation with other moms (there is a group of us who regularly meet at parks) who are almost always complaining about their kid's eating habits. Sameer will have nothing to do with your meals and is only interested in playing *peek-a-boo* with you. This really infuriates me. Why should only I be disliked?

16th September

You have given me the best birthday gift (belated though) ever! Today morning you said *Ma* (for the first time and that too while looking at me with melting little eyes. I was so overcome with emotion). Felt my heart reach out to you. Was looking forward to this moment so much! In fact on my birthday the day before, I kept standing by your side all the time, just hoping that you would say this most magical word of words. However, it was to be today you decided to give me this reason to be joyful.

I made you keep repeating it till you got bored and crawled away. Sameer kept staring at you and when he heard you say' *ma*, he tried to make you say *pa* too, but to no avail. You would only say *ma-ma* and you seemed thrilled with the response you got from us. Thank you so much.

30th September

Just recovered from a splitting headache. They seem to be pretty frequent now; I guess it is because of my irregular sleeping hours, you still get up in the middle of the night every now and then. Today though, the reason for it could be the argument I had with your *dadi.*

I can't really call it an argument because in case of one, it takes two to argue. In this instance I was just listening while she was doing all the talking. What actually happened was that your dad had asked for *masala dosas* for breakfast. However it slipped my mind while I was fussing over your food (and not "conveniently forgotten" as I was wrongly accused by my MIL later on). So when Sameer came to the dining table and saw *upma* (which he really dislikes) he threw a tantrum. Why did he have to do this? He is not really fussy about food and is ok with almost anything being served to him. I guess he was upset about his wishes not being given importance and then stupidly decided to crib and complain to his mom. Having told all his sob stories about how no one seems to care anymore for him he left for work (mind you after having three helpings of the *upma*). As a result I had to face your *dadi*'s ire regarding my 'carelessness' vis-à-vis chores, the family and Sameer in particular. I did manage to say that it is not as if I was resting or partying but looking after my kid. However a long list of "in my time we used to do this and that" followed. Initially I cried a lot (in my room) but after pondering over the situation realized that it is probably true that I had neglected my responsibilities towards my family. *Dadi* is not a stereotypical MIL who just keeps waiting to point out her *bahu's* shortcomings. So criticism coming from her definitely needs looking into. It is not as if I am just a mom, I have a more diverse role to play too. Hats off to working women. Do not know how they manage to juggle so many roles. Guess now it is time to take charge of the situation. But not before I give Sameer a piece of my mind for creating such a scene over *masala dosa's.*

8th October

Life sure has been hectic the past few days. In between cooking (yes I have taken charge of the kitchen much to Radha *maasi*'s amusement), supervising the customary *Diwali* housekeeping (now that is a whole different story all together), running behind you and dealing with vendors and the help, I somehow managed to find some time for your birthday preparations. Yes sweetheart, you are about to turn a YEAR OLD!

Time sure flies. It seems like yesterday that you came into our world and now you will cut your first birthday cake. The celebrations will take place in our beautiful garden lawn. I have zeroed in on a fairy tale theme which seems to be perfect for my darling prince. Have a big to do list

1. Select caterers
2. Hire an event management company
3. Decide on the cake.
4. Arrange for the return gifts
5. Choose your birthday outfit
6. Prepare the guest list and select a birthday invite.

I am very excited about your birthday. I want it to be perfect. There should be no room for any shortcomings. Just yesterday I was speaking to your *nana* about Simar *maasi*'s wedding preparations. He was pretty stressed out about the amount of planning required and spoke about the never ending list of things that need to be done "I understand papa, I too am going through an equal amount of planning for Vatsal's birthday party and am I stressed out. I can relate to what you are going through. Right now we are both sailing in the same boat".

He hung up with a snicker.

What?

Nowadays planning a birthday is not child's play (no pun intended).

Anyway I am still pretty angry with your dad and have let him know in no uncertain terms by serving him *masala dosas* five times (would have made it every day had my MIL not intervened) the last week. Every time he apologizes I serve him another *dosa.*

15th October

My purse got STOLEN!

Feels weird. Never thought it would happen to me.

This is so hard to come to terms with. This may sound *filmi* but it actually happened. I was shopping for your birthday party returns gifts on Brigade road. I kept drifting from shop to shop and the packets in my hand kept growing. I could not even dump it anywhere (the car wasn't around as the driver was on errand). The LV bag was making my shoulder ache and so to relieve myself, tucked it in the safety of one of my packets. It was only when I looked for my purse to pay for a pair of gorgeous shoes (they were to die for) that to my utmost horror and dismay I found my LV missing. Panic and hysteria gripped me. Standing on the pavement I kept looking through all the packets repeatedly but to no avail. I was about to break down into tears. How on earth could this happen to me? My cell too was in the bag.

Went to a nearby shop and called Sameer from there. As usual your dad never bothered to take the call. He never attends calls from unknown numbers. I've told him a zillion times that some emergency might arise anytime and just because of this stupid theory of his I might not be able to contact him. Goddamn it!

Next dialed *dadi*'s number and she calmly handled the situation. She immediately directed Suresh *bhaiya* to pick me up from the shop I called from. I left for home feeling very downcast (well you see the chauffeur was not carrying enough money on him for me to pick up the shoes that I had set my eyes on). Papa and Sameer were also home and then started a barrage of questions.

"When did it happen?"

"Between the bakery and the shoe shore."

"Did you see anyone take the bag out?" trust your dad to come up with the most asinine of questions. Would I not have created a scene had I 'seen someone taking my bag'? But since this was not a situation to be a smartass, I quietly shook my head.

"How much money were you carrying?"

"I left home with about 25000".

"But you would have spent some of it or a lot of it seeing the number of bags you are carrying."

I then took out all the bills from the packets and started to calculate and in the meantime Sameer got my number blocked and asked for another sim.

Well after totaling the amount spent on clothes, accessories, cosmetics, night wear, bathroom slippers, a shower curtain and two different sets of tiffin cases, the amount comes up to Rs 23,610.

"So you have lost about 1390. It is O.K! Don't worry and get upset about it."

"I am not upset about the money. I lost all my contacts just before the party and worst of all it was the brand new Louis Vuitton bag which mummy bought from Canada." Well that did shock everyone, but since there was no use crying over spilt milk the issue was laid to rest.

"By the way weren't you shopping for Vatsal's party?"

I sheepishly replied "Did I not get the sample tiffin boxes for you all to select?"

25th October

Why the hell did I have to lose my phone? I feel so handicapped without all my contacts.

To be honest *dadi* and Sameer have helped provide a lot of numbers but there are still so many more missing. I am so stressed about the party. Issuing invites, speaking to everyone, coordinating with the event manager, selecting the return gifts, arranging for a photographer...... God, the list seems never ending.

There is hardly any time left for you after all these exhausting activities. You are mostly with Kajal *maasi*. Your dad often jokes about her being more important in my life than him. I reply by telling him that he can trade places with her and again win the numero uno position from me. That sure shuts him up. Did I ever tell you that you have the cutest dimpled smile ever? Especially when you grin after doing something naughty. Like yesterday when you spilt the entire bowl of custard over your legs and squealed in delight. Seeing your smiling face makes it so difficult to be angry with you (and also because it was partially my own mistake for keeping the bowl within your reach).

When you crawl into my lap with a big smile just to hug me tight, it appears that the world momentarily consists of just the two of us. Nobody else exists or matters. At that moment it is only you and me and everything else is inconsequential. The party is being held day after, on a Sunday because I wanted to spend your actual birthday on the 1st of November with just you.

1st November

You look like an absolute angel when you sleep. The long brown curls softy fall all around your cheeks and forehead. Your chubby hands are clasping your favourite teddy. The parted rosy lips are a contrast to your fair cheeks. You are adorable. I could just watch you like this for hours and still not tire.

HAPPY BIRTHDAY sweetie!

You are now a year old. Today was a real contrast compared to the day of your party. It was a huge success. Everything went smoothly and as planned. Even the weather did not play truant. All the 150 odd guests had a great time and almost everyone messaged me about this being an awesome event. Well I am glad all the hard work paid off, but you actually enjoyed today far more. We did not fuss with your food today and gave you whatever you asked for.

We went to a temple and then an orphanage where we made you distribute clothes and books to all the children there. It was a somber reminder to see such disparity in the world. Here you were a single child with every possible luxury and there were these fifty odd orphans who did not even have the most basic necessities of life. There was a 6 year old girl who was constantly crying and upon being questioned told me in between sobs that she did not have a mother and to please get her one the next time I visited.

The tears ....took a long time to stop and I decided to start frequenting this orphanage a lot more. I intend to try everything within my means to help provide them with better facilities.

I would like you to always feel compassion and adopt a generous attitude towards those who are not as fortunate as you. What is the use of us having plenty if we cannot share it with the needy? From a very small age *nana* would take all of us to orphanages and old age homes. We would frequent it on a regular basis and not just on birthdays. Not only would we distribute necessities, but we also spent time with them.

Nana always encouraged us to be philanthropic, saying that giving would make us feel far richer and happier than receiving. It actually does. The smiles on the faces of the orphans and the heartfelt blessings of the aged always made us happier than getting many generous gifts from friends and relatives. I would secretly cry at the plight of these children and pray that God always kept them safe and sound. Very often anger would get the better of me when I would hear stories of the elderly being abandoned by their children because they now seemed to be more of a financial burden. It is probably as low as someone can go. How is it possible for people to abandon the parents who gave birth to them, nurtured them and made them self -sufficient? Today when these same parents have become infirm and need the support of those very children, the kids turn their backs on them in their hour of greatest need. *Nana* would ask me never to judge but to be the one to provide the healing balm. I would like to pass on the same values to you my son.

Your birthday celebrations continue and we then headed for an amusement Park where you had hours of joyful fun.

Next stop was the Bannerghatta zoo where you were overjoyed on seeing all the various exotic fauna, reserving the most amount of delight for the implacable elephants. However the trip to the zoo had to be cut short because it was at that point when you decided to take your daily nap.

The day ended with you cutting a cake (most of which was smeared on your face) and playing with the toys *nana* & *nani* sent you; a tricycle, the one which I can push, a huge car to get your F1 driving skills honed, a swing which you took an instant liking to (God alone know where I will keep it), a desk and chair. This did not leave me with too many choices as to what to get you. We finally decided to get a fixed deposit done in your name. Sounds boring but is a very practical gift.

5th November

Now the focus shifts to Simar *maasi*'s wedding which is coming up on the 12th of next month. I will be leaving for Kolkata in a couple of weeks and there is tons to be done before that. Have to coordinate what everyone would be wearing.

A few silk and kanjivaram sarees and silk bedcovers have to be picked up for her trousseau, it is one thing which Bangalore can claim to be unmatched in (other than the fabulous weather of course).

Diwali is fast approaching. Your first one. Lots of cleaning yet to be done and sweets to be sent across to friends and relatives. Will be sending chocolates across to all my friends (who eats sweets now in these times?).

Housewife's work never seems to end. It is a 24/7 job which comes with no perks, holidays, allowances etc. and you are always taken for granted. I too want to start my own venture but it will have to wait till you start going to school. I also want to claim to be something other than a homemaker each time I fill a form. Doesn't everyone want to achieve something and prove themselves? I am no different. Sameer is quite understanding and supportive about it, especially since I am ready to wait till you start schooling.

No point discussing it now as there is still plenty of time for that and right now there is enough as it is on my plate.

16th November

Last week, *Diwali* was a blast. We burst so many crackers (you were not a part of it since you were howling and clinging to Kajal *maasi* each time a loud noise was heard) that it did not come as a surprise when Malhotra uncle from the adjacent bungalow came and requested us to 'please' cut down on the racket as it was too much for him. We readily obliged as his request was appropriate and we had almost exhausted our store of crackers anyway.

We visited the orphanage and distributed sweets, crackers and a new toy to each child. *Dada* was very moved and asked me to come here with the whole family on all important occasions.

You remember me mentioning about the little girl who asked me to get her a mother? Her name is Priya and her parents were laborers who died in an accident a couple of years back. Since then she has been living here. I gave her a small portable radio and spent plenty of time listening to her talk. There was a tiny smile on her face when we left. She waved a cheerful goodbye but not before she asked me when was I visiting next.

Very soon I assured her.

This left us not only with a warm sensation but also proved to be a very humbling experience. Sameer tried to put up a brave front and said that this is how life was and it was not always fair, but I could see that he had been deeply touched. Why can't he show his emotions ever? It is alright for a man to *cry* and be moved about something that's deeply emotional.

He however just does not subscribe to this view. Men don't cry, he says. Well I would like to rest my case by asking him why God gave them tear ducts in their eyes?

We had to be extra careful with you at home because there were *diyas* in every nook and corner and all you wanted to do was grab them. It was only when you fell asleep that we all let out a collective sigh of relief. Coming up next is a trip to Kolkata.

25th November

A house with a wedding going on is so much of fun. There is excitement, tension, chaos, merriment and hordes of relatives pouring in from all corners. Met cousins, tried out new restaurants, while *nani* kept chiding me and talked about the ill effects of outside food. You have not yet been weaned so I am not really free to eat whatever I like (specifically, things your *nani* hates).

Everybody is talking about how slim I look and the best part is that they all have (almost all) the same wonderful thing to tell me.

"Oh my God! You have lost so much of weight."

"Is that really you?"

"Wow! You are looking perfect."

"I am jealous of your figure."

"You are so lucky. You can eat all that you want without a care in the world."

Now these are words which every girl wants to hear and she can never get tired of hearing them. This makes all the sacrifices so worth it. YES! Have returned to my pre pregnancy size. Hurrah!

I was enjoying it so much. Finally I was fat free and comfortable with my body again.

There are however always a few aunts who have a cynical viewpoint.

"Oh you have become a bit too thin."

"You have started looking pale? How on earth did you knock off all that fat?"

"Simran beta have you got yourself checked? This kind of

weight loss is not healthy. You are actually looking sick", and "how weak you have become."

Trust *nani* to have to say it. Nowadays, the whole world is trying to slim down to size zero and here I was naturally blessed with it without having to put in any real effort. The best part was that I was eating exactly what I loved. I guess my metabolism was on overdrive. That is the only rational explanation that I could come up with. Yes I do confess feeling weak and giddy at times, but that's just a natural outcome of watching one's weight.

There was this relative of an aunt of mine who came up with the most ridiculous of all comments. "You are looking dreadfully thin. Is everything ok between you and your husband?"

Now try to figure it out. Like all the marital problems in the world are meant only for thin couples.

Getting back to you, the transition has not been so smooth for you this time. So many unfamiliar faces and everyone wants to hold you which disconcerts and scares you, making you cling harder to me. It is pretty tiring to have you dangling on my arm all the time. Ravi *mama* has nicknamed you *Koala bear.* Come to think of it, you are indeed hanging on to me like a baby Koala. However, I thankfully don't look like one anymore.

I know it is a new setting for you and that you are not taking kindly to all the aunts (what is it with these aunts who make it a point to arrive early to help out, but only end up shopping and socializing instead) wanting to play with your cheeks or question you as if you are supposed to answer them.

Simar *maasi* is looking beautiful. Actually she was always very pretty so I should now be using the term gorgeous. Her glowing complexion was courtesy all the spa treatments and a diet which consists of mostly fruits and juices. I could never follow such a diet though. I am too much of a foodie to give it all up and as you can now see, I don't need to either.

Nana, *nani* and Ravi all look extremely tired thanks to all their exertions to pull off a big fat, Indian wedding. There has not been much where I could help with though. The trousseau has already been packed. The gifts for Aakash are placed over decorative trays and all the jewelry to be given to everyone including Simar is neatly packed in boxes and labeled. The catering is being looked after by a team of well- trained cooks, so any interference in the kitchen is ruled out. All the goodies and knick knacks to be placed in the rooms of the *baraatis* have been packed in exquisite silk pouches and kept safely away. That does not really leave much for me to do except pretend to be as busy as the others. I loved her trousseau, incidentally. The designer sarees and suits are a treat to the eye. Her western wear inspires me to shrink a few more inches to fit in them and her accessories are to die for. I will not even get to her jewelry which actually made me envious, but there is one item which does not evoke pangs of jealously.

Her footwear - each and every pair is a flat. None of it even has a trace of a heel. She can't walk around in heels with Aakash, since she already seems to appear a little taller. I would however never trade them for my stilettos and pencil heels.

You may be wondering why on earth I am describing the trousseau to you. You definitely wouldn't be interested if you feel anything like your dad. Last night when I was narrating it to Sameer, he yawned a few times, tried to change the topic and finally pointedly asked me if there was nothing better to talk about. Sheesh! Men, hard to figure them out and they always make it appear like it's the other way round.

I am off to practice for the sangeet; I will be dancing for two songs. *Taare hain baarati* with Sameer and *Saajan ji ghar aaye* with my cousins.

Don't know whether I was dancing or laughing or both. Especially during the part where all the men are supposed to lift us women. Gaurav was my partner and each time he had to lift me up, he had an expression of mock fright and went *itni shakti hamein dena data ki Simran ko utha sake hum.* Had he not been my favorite cousin, I would have punched the daylights out of him. We all sang *phoolon ka taaron ka* as the finale. Ravi was to sing the entire song and the rest of were supporting him in the chorus. Ravi feels that we don't sing but croak and a single chorus was enough to test the audience's patience.

Nani got misty eyed every now and then. And before you knew it, my aunts, cousin sisters and I joined in. The guys were putting on a very brave face but I know it won't last forever.

2nd December

Sameer arrived yesterday! So very happy to see him. My grin stretched from ear to ear much to the amusement of Priya who teased me about it. Apparently I was blushing so much that my cheeks resembled a beetroot. Talk about stretching the truth.

He was lavished with so much attention from everyone that it got to a point where he wished it would stop. Food, food and yet some more food. It seemed as if food was the only language my *bhua*'s and chachi's knew in terms of showing their affection for someone. *Gajar, badam, dal ka halwas* the type where a thick layer of *ghee* was floating on top, was fed to him with every meal. Your dad developed a distinct fear of my aunts as a result of these ministrations. We started practicing for our duet *Taare hain baarati* amidst, cheers, whistles and 'so cute, soooo sweet', comments. That soon changed however to "*Jiju* you are forgetting your steps", "*Jiju* do not stamp your foot", "you are supposed to dance and not march", "your face should be more expressive", "you look as if Simran has died, no that would actually be one of pure bliss" and other much more critical observations. The last comment though wasn't very funny.

It was difficult if not impossible teaching your dad to shake a leg. Thank God he is just dancing to one song. Simar put up a video of him dancing on Facebook (which he has still not forgiven her for) and it has already received 62 comments. Facebook is a blessing and boon for all of us. No matter which part of the world your family and friends are in it helps you to stay connected to all of them. It is a common ground to interact with friends and peek into their lives while showcasing ours too. Let everyone know what is happening with regular updates (but I would like to confess that is very annoying to get hourly petty updates from friends whom you haven't met for decades).

You were thrilled to bits to see Sameer and refused to let go of him. I had no complaints with this arrangement (finally, my very aching arms would get some well-deserved rest) but Simar was pretty upset since you had just started to take a liking to her.

Our bouts of frequent crying had now turned into full blown weeping sessions. I can't show you my true feelings because you start hollering as soon as you see me shedding tears. We are shifting to a bungalow situated nearby. It's already difficult with so many relatives here. Nonetheless we were enjoying every minute of this experience. We were making such a racket that the elders had to reprimand us.

This felt like childhood again. We didn't mind it but were wary of actually having the elders join in. I am living every moment to the fullest. Haven't had so much fun in ages. Don't remember when I last laughed so much.

8th December

Vatsal I love you so very much. Thank you so much for everything. You're the reason my world is so perfect. I never knew that it was possible to feel the kind of love that I feel for you. Today I have this funny feeling of really cherishing all these memories.

I have this strange sensation of everything drifting by….

Like leaves floating away in a random breeze. I cannot explain this feeling to anyone because I myself do not understand it. Time moves on, but I wish I could forever savor these moments. Feels like everyone and everything here was bidding me adieu, like I would never see them again. Wanted to soak in as much as I could, as if it wouldn't be there for me anymore. I feel like I would be taken very far from it all. It was a fleeting sensation though and I held on to you not wanting to let go.

I guess I was feeling very emotional, anyway have to get back to my dance practices and have another laughing session at your father's expense.

9th December

We have shifted to a huge bungalow. The spacious rooms all have sofas in them and a small fridge. The bathrooms are very roomy which suits you just fine. Right now though, you would be hard-pressed to differentiate it from a busy railway station platform with suitcases scattered everywhere and trays containing food in every nook and cranny. Shirts and sarees, baby stuff, slippers and shoes all just lying around. In short, a total mess. Had your *dadi* been here she would have sorted it out in a jiffy. She will be here with *dada* tomorrow.

The *baraat* is coming on the afternoon of the 11th and will be staying in the same five star hotel where the wedding also is being held. It is a new hotel and I love the way they have used water for landscaping and decoration. You too like the idea though you want to play in it (which does become a little embarrassing).

There is a real buzz in the air. Everybody is really busy. Almost everyone has been allocated a small responsibility (*nana* says you need to do it to give everyone a sense of purpose and make them feel like they belong). We all eagerly await the arrival of the *baraat*. *Nana* hasn't slept properly in days. He just manages to shut his eyes for a couple of hours in the night and that too on *nani*'s insistence.

Why can't weddings be a relaxed affair so that the family members too can have a good time and let their hair down? I remember *nana* being ill for days, exhausted after my wedding and it seems that he is going to follow suit this time too. Ravi and Sameer seem to be doing no better and it is still three more days to the wedding. Everybody is already so stressed and the *baraat* hasn't even arrived yet.

You play a lot with Pinku's son and Amit *bhaiya*'s daughter. They are 6 and 7 respectively and love to look after you. You children are the only immediate family members who don't have their foreheads crinkled in increasing worry lines.

Not even yesterday, when Shagun *dadi*, your *nana*'s *maasi* had severe pain in her chest. We assumed a heart attack, and the panic button was pressed. It was utter chaos for the next three hours; everyone ran helter-skelter instead of deciding upon the next course of action. Four cars carrying *6 uncles, 4 aunties, 5 brothers and 3 bhabhi's* arrived at a nearby clinic. Most of us had to wait in the lobby as the receptionist reminded them gently that this was a hospital and not a fish market. Two long hours later, after a battery of tests it turned out to only be a gastric problem. So everyone returned home with a long list of instructions for Shagun *dadi* to follow, she sure had everyone scared.

18th December

Back in Bangalore! I have left with a very heavy heart. Simar's *vidaai* had created a void in everyone's hearts and brought tears to all of us. *Nani* was inconsolable. *Nana* and Ravi wept silently away from the prying eyes.

From the day a daughter is born in our country, we talk only about her marriage. As she grows, the elders want her to learn things, telling her *Ye sab cheesen shaadi ke baad bahut kaam ayengi.* When she throws tantrums she is told *Gussa kam kiya karo, Shaadi ke baad saas ke saamne ye tevar nahi chalenge.* When she grows into youth, parents start searching for a suitable groom to send her on her way. Yet when the day of reckoning arrives, emotions get the better of us. Every *vidaai* will see the girl's family left disconsolate. The sobs and tears do not end. The pain in your chest refuses to fade away. It is so difficult to handover the apple of your eye to another family.

This was a classic example of that; we had planned for this occasion, months on end, but when the day finally dawned all those dammed emotions burst through. *Nani* looked so devastated.

Getting back to happier thoughts, it was indeed a dream wedding. Everything went as planned. Except for one tiny incident, I don't even know if it is worth mentioning. While dancing to *Saajan ji ghar aaye,* I slipped. I luckily did not fall as Gaurav caught me in time, but my slipper flew and hit somebody on the knee in a manner resembling something from the *Matrix.* This person, believe it or not, was none other than your dad. His face was a mask of frozen surprise. Since not too many people had witnessed this incident, we carried on with our dance as if nothing had happened and I made sure I did not look Sameer in the eye. Of course I was to hear no end of this episode later. "Are you sure that it was an accident".

"How on earth will I live this down, publically being beaten up by my wife?"

"Did you by any chance aim for my head?" I will not be able to show my face again". His sad jokes have continued till today and going on by the looks of it, will do for some more years to come.

Relatives from both sides spoke very highly of all the arrangements. The food, the décor, the gifts, the *sangeet*, all received rave reviews. All our hard work finally paid off. Guests left lavishing high praise, which was very satisfying. I was the last one to leave.

Now coming to you, all was not hunky dory. You had a slight fever (I repeat slight, less than 100) but behaved like you were in tremendous agony. I guess you are like your dad, always craving for attention. You went to no one else. Not even Kajal *maasi. Dada* and *dadi* too tried to bribe you with lollipops but to no avail. You clung on to me all the time. You hardly ate any of your meals and kept crying for milk. I had to keep going to the washroom to feed you, which was not an easy task wearing the heavy sarees and elaborate jewelry. I guess the time has come to wean you off milk and will start working on it from this fortnight itself.

I wanted to stay longer with *nani* and *nana*, you see they were really upset and I could sense their loneliness. Having you stay back would have eased their pain, but *dadi* was already missing you way too much and wanted you back as soon as possible. Even Sameer asked me to now come back home. So here we are- back home.

Before I forget to mention it, Simar and Aakash have gone to New-Zealand for their honeymoon.

23rd December

I have had a torrid time trying to wean you. You howl day and night especially when you see me. I try not to come near you. You lookout for me and say *mama-mama* repeatedly. It is not very difficult to distract you during the day but is far more problematic in the night. I am sleeping in the guestroom but I can I can hear your wails through the night. I have to do everything in my power to stop myself from taking you in my arms. Sameer and *dadi* took turns rocking you to sleep. You were tempted with new toys but the ploy didn't work. You even refuse to touch your sipper. It is been three days since we began this process.

You are almost 14 months and we decided that now was the ideal time to wean you off. But I can promise you that I have regretted this decision each time your plaintive cries fell to my ears. Yesterday night I wept along with you and prayed that you would get over this.

25th December

Merry Christmas sweetheart! You have finally stopped protesting. You still get up and do cry a little but are now content with your sipper and don't throw a tantrum. Motherhood is so strange. All this while I kept hoping that you would be weaned off soon but now when you actually are I feel a void. Sameer sighs and says that there is no pleasing women.

I or rather Santa Claus gifted you a blanket (he left it under your pillow). Sameer found it very funny that I actually hid a blanket under your pillow but I wanted you to be all excited and surprised. Alright I know I was expecting a lot out of a one year old and yes it was too early for you to believe in Santa, but I enjoyed pretending to be surprised and pulling out a package followed by a series of exclamations on seeing your gift. You were completely unmoved and did not show any signs of joy on seeing the gift I had so lovingly selected for you. Before you start wondering as to why I chose a blanket as your gift (I agree that you already have far more than you need); it is only because of your *dadi.* She forbade me from buying any more bulky presents for you. She isn't really to be blamed for her decision. Every nook and cranny of our house is stuffed with toys. Your swings, bouncer, slide, prams, cycles, portable car (which is huge) are interspersed by soft toys which seem to keep appearing out the blue.

I swore I've been clearing them up and so does Kajal *maasi*, but they mysteriously seem to reappear again. Not that they have any specific storage spot. They are usually dumped in both the guest rooms and I keep hoping that *dadi* does not walk into those rooms. So it was very fair on her part to ask me (actually it was more of a command) to buy something small and useful and only if absolutely necessary.

She needn't have accused me regarding your growing pile of toys. Most of them have been gifted. Come to think of it almost all it actually, I hardly have time to shop nowadays.

Correction. I hardly have time for anything these days. I don't sit endlessly in front of the television except to play rhymes for you during your meal times. No long chats on the phone; it is more like 'hello' followed by 'I have to hang up now' within a couple of minutes. Visits to the spa have long been forgotten; even basic necessities at the parlour seem like luxuries now. Let's not even get into the topic of shopping. The less said about it the better.

All this is beside the point though. I got you a very special blanket. It is printed with our photographs. There is a large print of the two us in the center and the borders are done with images of everybody else. Sameer cribbed so much about not being in that main image with us.

28th December

You've finally started WALKING!

I am so excited, no, make that ecstatic!

I am on top of the world; beyond this, words fail me. Sameer missed this big moment (but I did manage to record it on my cell phone). I am elated today. Your first few steps are such a big milestone for me. You rose up unsteadily, took an experimental step, unsure of what you were doing, balanced yourself, looked at my anxious face once and then bravely started to walk before falling down. Your first five baby steps. You were thrilled at your achievement or maybe my excitement rubbed off on to you and were clapping in glee. You made a few more attempts (for the benefit of the camera) before regressing back into the crawling mode. I called up your *nana*, *nani*, Ravi mama, even Simar *maasi*. Everyone was absolutely thrilled with the exception of Simar *maasi* and Aakash (can't really blame them, it was 3 am in NZ). Sameer was glad to hear the news but said he would not make it home due to a lot of work related commitments. Honestly speaking I was initially a bit disappointed. He could have come just for a little while to see your magnum opus, but I thought later that it was good that he couldn't since you refused to walk again for the rest of the day. I will now sign off for today and retire early. Nowadays I seem to tire very easily.

1st January 2005

Happy New Year my love! May this year bring you endless joy and keep you in the best of health. We all had a family dinner (food from a restaurant; I obviously did not want to cook on New Year's Eve). Nothing else could be done; by the time Sameer and *dada* arrived home, it was almost midnight (this period is also the phase for sales).

Yesterday we went to visit a relative of mummy. She is your *dadi*'s cousin sister. I could never really stand her and if given a choice would never have bothered to visit her, but I didn't have any say in the matter. We had to take the stairs to her 4th floor apartment as there was no elevator. I generally pride myself in being able to climb up to six floors without exerting myself too much, but yesterday by the time I reached her flat I was absolutely breathless and was swept by a wave of giddiness. I had to lie down while she droned at *dadi.*

"These girls now days, I tell you, are such delicate darlings. No stamina at all. Imagine not being able to climb a few floors. What is this generation coming upon?"

"No Rachna, actually she just started her cycle today so she is feeling drained out", fibbed mummy, wondering why I tire so easily nowadays.

15th January

Just recovered from a week long fever. Feeling drained out as I had a temperature of 102 degrees for 4 days. The doctor thought it was probably a viral fever which is going around now. Come to think of it, whenever someone is down with fever, doctors generally say that it is a viral fever doing the rounds currently and they happen to say it all year round.

I hardly got to see you fearing I would infect you. You did not seem to mind and were engrossed in playing with your innumerable toys. It is probably a very selfish comment but I did feel hurt that you could manage without me. I laughed at Sameer's jokes about me needing you more than you depending on me, but I was personally afraid. Would a time really come when you would stop needing me? I dread to think of it.

I am much better now. Though still very weak. I think I have lost a little too much weight (imagine me writing this).

"Don't worry love; once you start eating normally it will all bounce back."

Seriously your dad!

18th February

Haven't yet regained my strength. Still tire out very easily. Guess it is because of the weight loss. Can't say I am complaining about it. Consuming all the desserts and deep fried items, which are sinfully rich in calories, without a care in the world.

This might actually be a dream come true. Maybe there is justice in this world after all.

I was looking forward to seeing you walk, but now when you can run, I miss the period when you simply sat. You just don't want to remain still. One moment here and another moment there. No wonder I feel exhausted all the time.

Sameer has suggested a holiday for just the two of us. Now that you are weaned he feels that we leave you behind with *dada*, *dadi* and Kajal *maasi*. It is probably because of my very tepid response to his birthday and Valentine's Day. Where did I have the time or energy to organize anything for him? But yes he is right about us needing to spend some quality time with each other.

Hmmmm.... a whole week of relaxation is not a bad idea, with leaving you behind being the only downside. Anyway the holiday is still in the planning stage.

25th February

Yes it's all done. Bookings made, packing complete and tears too have started flowing. I can't stop crying. This is the first time I am leaving you behind.

Will you miss me? Would you ask for me? Would my sudden disappearance upset you?

"Oh God! Stop acting like a primadonna. We are going to a resort and spa which is just a 45 minute drive from home. If he misses you, we will be back in a jiffy or he can simply join us."

Maybe he did have a point there. We are only going for four nights and yes it is less than an hour away from home. Keeping my fear of leaving you behind in mind, he planned on a nearby resort. Alright, but why does everyone feel I am over reacting?

4th March

I had such a great time. It was such a wonderful holiday. A much needed break. Finally, we both got some together time. We spoke at length about each other which was a change from having to constantly talk about you.

Sameer discussed his ambitions about growing his chain and taking it to new cities. He now wants to make his retail stores accessible in most of the cities across the country. We joked, we laughed except when he made fun of my appetite- that was not funny as usual.

"Are you sure you do not have a thyroid issue or something?

You are piling on food but there is no trace of it on you. Where is all the fat going? What is the secret behind your continuous weight reduction?" I think he is jealous. Not that he needs to be. He can still fit into his college clothes (he has a couple of jeans from his college days which he still easily manages to get into).

I did miss you terribly but heard from *dadi* that you were getting along just great. I am thankful for that but had this stupid nagging feeling that you were angry with me for leaving you behind. I needn't have worried though, the moment you saw me, you ran straight into my arms and smiled wonderfully. So much for my apprehensions!

"By the way love, your dress seems to be a little too large for you."

I glanced down and realized that my dress was indeed quite loose, which was surprising since it had been a snug fit, just a couple of months ago.

30th April

Bangalore is hot. God, the heat is UNBEARABLE. It is around 33 degrees. Heat is one thing I really cannot stand. This is the first time I felt this burning sensation all over me. The weather here, if not always pleasant isn't inhospitable either. The really funny thing however was that I was the only one feeling the heat. *Dadi* is getting a little annoyed with me complaining about it all the time. There were times when I felt the heat literally sapping away my energy.

I am not exaggerating, a couple of days back while waiting for the car to come out of the parking lot I almost passed out. It was such an uncomfortable feeling. First, I started feeling breathless and then my head began to spin. My vision became blurred and hazy. Fortunately the car arrived at the nick of time and I gratefully flopped into the back seat. No more shopping in the afternoons for me.

10th May

Apparently Ravi *mama* has a soft corner for someone. Her name is Anushka and she is the daughter of your *nana's* friend. Now with proposals coming in and with *nani-nana* seriously thinking about his marriage, he candidly confessed his feelings to us. This news was initially unexpected, but we had to acknowledge that he had made a smart choice. She is good looking (have met her a few times in social get-togethers), homely, well educated (she is currently in her final year of M.B.A) comes from a well-established family, who, to make matters really easy, are from our own community. In short, a perfect match. Both families know each other very well. So what were we waiting for? Her final exams will take place in July so we'll wait for them to finish. Wow I am going to get a bhabhi real soon.

By the way Kajal *maasi* has taken leave for a month. If I could, I wouldn't let her go but then she really did not give me much of an option. It is going be a very long month without her.

14th May

Had a long discussion with Sameer yesterday. Guess why? To plan a sibling for you. I know you are not yet two but I don't want much of an age gap between you children. I want to raise you both together. Sameer was so glad to hear it. He is keen on having a large family (a view I do not subscribe to). He felts that three kids were a must and then he had the cheek to prefix that with an "at least".

I understand that he might've had a lonely childhood with him being an only child, but three kids in this day and age? You have got to be kidding me. Had to put an end to that line of thought and very firmly and finally said.

"Hum do hamare do."

"Simi, why should we not have three kids? We are young; we can afford it and have plenty of family support. Do you not want to provide Vatsal the joy of two siblings?"

"Give it a rest. I have to go through the pregnancies, the labour and post labour normalization and it does not end at that. Every single day I run behind Vatsal, juggling various duties irrespective of all the help that we have. Multiplying that another two-fold would be unmanageable. It is already extremely tiring Sameer."

"OK now don't get upset. It was just an idea of mine. Let's meet Sudha aunty once and I hope that its twins this time.

He seriously doesn't know when to give up.

18th May

Had to have a blood test done finally. Couldn't delay it anymore. Have been trying to avoid it like crazy but everybody seems convinced that I am anemic, so the test is now mandatory. Shouldn't really make such a big deal about it. After all what is a needle prick for someone who has gone through labour?

Six small bottles of blood were drawn out of my protesting body. The number of tests prescribed exceeded the number of questions asked in an examination. The reason was that I had *fainted* yesterday.

Don't be alarmed, it was just for about ten minutes (Sameer was visibly shaken when he said that it was the longest ten minutes of his life). I was feeling very tired (no Kajal *maasi* remember) and when I was trying to feed you, I passed out.

Fortunately it was early morning and everybody was at home. I came around shortly, but the damage was done. Everybody panicked. Believe it or not your *dadi* started crying. *Dada* himself went to fetch our family doctor. I assured them that I was ok and it was simply a bout of weakness but no one listened to me. Dr Sharma gave us a huge list of tests to be conducted and advised me complete rest with plenty of fluids.

"These girls today only want to diet; I do not understand the madness behind trying to be reed thin. Please see that she eats healthy food from now on. I will come again as soon as the reports arrive."

So today morning, the blood test was done on an empty stomach, urine sample collected and in some time I have to go through an X-ray and ultra sound (though I am yet to understand the need for that). You are to be with *dadi* for the day while Sameer and I will have to go to the diagnostic center. Hope you are on your best behavior today. I have a feeling that I might be pregnant. I am showing all the symptoms. I do hope so.

20th May

Sameer is acting pretty weird. He has not gone to work from the past three days. He's been perpetually glued to the phone or on the net for long periods. He says that he is gearing up for some legal problems that are coming up regarding one of our prime properties, but that shouldn't be such a big reason for everyone in the house to be upset.

Dadi too sports a worried frown, only you my sweetie pie still seem untouched by all this mysterious anxiety. Nowadays, all you want to do is pick things up and smash them. The loud noises make you smile and dance in glee. You do have some very cute dance moves, especially when you wiggle your bum. Life with you is such a contradiction of sorts. Time flies by when I am playing with you while it hardly seems to move when I have to run behind you to feed you. There is no one cuter than you (especially with your dimpled smile) and nobody infuriates me more than you when you are stubborn for some silly reason.

Giving you a bath is so much fun for the both of us. We create bubbles, splash water on each other, and have lots of toys in the tub, but taking you out of the warm water and then having to tolerate your crying is so exasperating.

All said and done however, you make life beautiful. You give me something to look forward to every moment. You give meaning to my existence. You have bought Sameer and me closer to each other. Gone are the days when we would fight over stupid issues. Now whenever we are together alone (which is very rare, thanks to you) we just talk, hold hands and enjoy each other's company. I wait for you to do something new, say words which you haven't said before, make really cute faces wrinkling your nose while closing your eyes when you sample a new dish and don't happen to like the taste. The best thing though, is when you are sleepy you hug me tightly. Then you curl up in my lap and fall asleep while I sing you a lullaby. I love and cherish that moment and could live forever in it.

In you I get to relive my childhood all over again. It is supposed to be the most memorable phase of our life, but unfortunately we are never able to properly recollect any of it. Your *nani* would often tell me stories of how I was as a child, and today I don't know why but I have a strong urge to share them with you. Mom tells me that I was a pretty well behaved kid (till I was about five and before we siblings decided to make fighting with each other our favorite pastime) and loved to play with dolls and blocks.

I loved dressing up and would spend hours in front of the mirror trying out various lipstick shades (which would be more lavishly applied on my cheeks than lips). I would love to hear stories and would pester her till she finally sat down to tell me one. I was very excited about the idea of going to school until I realized that *nani* would not be joining me and then would howl for days before finally getting used to the idea. Earlier, I would apparently be very possessive about both my parents and would not like the idea of having to share them with Ravi.

When Simar was born I was under the impression that I was getting a real doll to play with. It was a lot of fun up until she started crying. I even once even asked them to exchange her for a regular doll that would be easier to handle. I laugh now when I hear these anecdotes and hope to provide you with an equally happy childhood.

21st May

I have to go through the tests again! Can you believe it? The diagnostic center got a few names mixed up and I had to be one of them! Of all the rotten luck. How can they be so incompetent? Feel like suing them. Sameer assured me that he had personally yelled at them and we decided that we would never return to that center again. I will now be taking all the tests again at another diagnostic center. God why did this have to happen to me? Imagine going through those extensive tests again. I wanted to protest and throw a hissy fit, but he is already very anxious about the legal mess so I did not have the heart to refuse him. Besides it was not his fault. So here goes another day wasted in a series of tests.

22nd May

The entire day yesterday was spent in undergoing tests. After the blood test, I took an ultrasound which bought some disturbing news. Sameer informed me after speaking to the doctor who conducted it that there seems to be some blockage in the ovarian tubes. This might delay the next pregnancy. To confirm it, I needed to go through a pet/ CT scan. He spoke to Dr Sudha and we were immediately ushered in. However after the CT scan I was tired and sore as I had to lie still for more than two hours.

During all that time I repeatedly kept having negative thoughts about the blockage. What if it actually delayed my next pregnancy? Or in the worst possible scenario what if I could not conceive normally again? Would I also have to go through a million more tests and painful procedures? What if none of this could help me; then would Sameer's dream of a large family remain unfulfilled? What if this affects our relationship? I tried to stay away from negative thoughts but it was pointless, the further I pushed them away, the stronger they got. I guess I was jumping to conclusions. After all, this was just a small possibility and modern medicine always had a cure. There was absolutely nothing to stress myself over. After a really long and exhausting day, I looked forward to seeing your smiling face and boy did you oblige, you just ran straight into my arms and refused to let go. I love you Vatsal; love you a lot.

25th May

Had to get operated on yesterday. It all happened so fast that I had no time to think even. The doctor informed us that it had to been done immediately or else the tubes could get affected. It was a biopsy which lasted for half an hour and was done under local anesthesia. It was to remove the blockage in the tubes. Still in pain. Unable to write any more. I love you baby.

30th May

Vatsal I have a disease which takes a long time to recover from.

It is known as *ovarian cancer.*

I got to know about it day before from a heartbroken Sameer. My world came crashing around me. Couldn't believe my ears. Surely there had to be a mistake. I am too young to be affected by it. How could this happen to me?

"Sameer you are lying, please tell me you are lying. DAMN YOU SAMEER! "

"Please tell me this is all just a bad joke, please, please, please." I ranted all day. I cried all night. I didn't know what to do, where to go. Oh God is this actually happening to me?

Sameer wants me to be strong. Everybody around me is asking me to be brave. I am however unresponsive. I am too shocked to react. How do I collect myself? What do I tell myself? I feel too numb to even think straight. Have never touched cigarettes, done drugs, had any exposure to radiation, or have any family history of cancer. I have never harmed or wished ill of anyone, then why is this injustice being meted out to me? I am so scared Vatsal. I don't know what will happen.

2nd June

I had a meeting with Dr. Shiv Shekhar one of Bangalore's leading gynecologic oncologist. He did not have happy news. The cancer has spread. It is now in the third stage. It generally prevalent in women in the age group of 45 years or more, but there are always exceptions to the norm.

Why did I have to be the exception?

"You have displayed all the classic symptoms. Significant weight loss, nausea, vomiting, abdominal pain, why didn't you get this checked earlier?"

Because Doctor I never in my wildest of dreams ever thought that I might become afflicted with this disease. Every time I lost a kg, I congratulated myself on my good fortune at being able to so easily lose the one thing that most people want to lose so badly.

I was planning on extending my family. Wanted to bring another bundle of joy into this world. I was so happy in my wonderful life, why would I think about dark clouds looming on the horizon? He kept droning in technical jargon but I had stopped listening. I was too stunned to be able to comprehend. Too numb to reply. Could just make out *go for chemotherapy immediately*.

He asked me to wait outside while he spoke to Sameer. I sat outside quietly thinking only about you.

Twenty minutes later Sameer emerged. He had a very brave smile plastered on his face.

"There is good news love. The doctor has assured us that chemotherapy will be able to control and fight the cancer. It is possible to remove it completely. Simi please let us do this together. You're going to fight it. You've got to do this. For me, for Vatsal, for us. We can do this Simi, we can."

I nodded robotically in agreement.

4th June

We consulted two more doctors. They had nothing new to add. Tomorrow morning we are heading to Mumbai. Sameer thinks they might be able to more confidently guarantee recovery. *Dada* wants us to go to America for the treatment while *dadi* feels that UK is a better option. Nobody however is asking me my opinion.

If they did, I would tell them that all I want to do is to be with you. Just you. I don't want to talk about any malady or its treatment. I just want to be by your side. Hear your half formed sentences, watch you hide things and laugh while watching me search for it and sing lullabies to you.

7th June

Doctors in Mumbai had the same thing to say. A couple of tests were repeated. I've stopped feeling anything now. Meanwhile reports had been sent to the doctors in Singapore, London and America. Tele conferencing is on. Dad and Sameer along with a couple of doctors are at it all time. They have informed my family in Kolkata. They are all reaching Bangalore tomorrow. A consensual decision will be taken together regarding the future course of action.

Nobody is saying it and no discussions are taking place and everyone remains hopeful, but what if............yes...........what if nothing worthwhile comes out of it? What if the cancer spreads beyond any hope of recovery? What if the medication fails?

There are many questions swirling in my mind but I don't find any convincing answers for them. I realize that Sameer seems to be talking to me. I haven't heard anything.

"Simi what do you propose?

Simi! Simi have you even heard what I am saying?"

My eyes do not move. They do not blink. I am staring ahead at nothing in particular. Finally I look at him and say.

"Please take me home. Home to my Vatsal. Just let me be with my baby."

I quietly walked out of the hospital.

10th June

Nani, *nana*, Ravi and Simar are here. They are all trying to behave normally. They are smiling, joking, discussing current affairs and my childhood stories. Pretending as if nothing has happened. Their eyes though say it all. I have heard the expression *saying it with your eyes*, but only now am I truly able to understand it. Their hearts are crying out and I can see it in their eyes. A tiny scratch on you Vatsal upsets me, so how can my predicament not affect them?

Mom, dad you don't need to say anything. I know it all. We are all being strong for each other's sake.

11th June

I am not going to give in. I will fight it and defeat it. I have to. For your sake Vatsal, I can't let it win. Why was I so lost all this while? I should have begun my fight much earlier. How could I even begin to think of succumbing to it? I am not a loser. There is too much at stake. Defeat is not even an option for me. I can do this. You gave me the strength I needed.

Today while I sat lost in my thoughts, you tripped and fell down. A tiny cut on your elbow bought tears in your eyes. You could not be pacified by anyone. Mummy! Mummy! Your eyes kept looking out for me. *Dadi*, *nani* no one would do. You saw me sitting in the corner and ran up to me and cried in my arms.

'Mummy got hurt'. Your cries woke me up from my introspective stupor. I hugged you and cried loudly. We both cried holding on to each other tightly. Both were scared of letting go. I realized that this cancer had to be defeated. You needed me. Not just to soothe these little cuts but for every step in life. Through all its ups and downs, you need me and no one else. I could not give up on you. You depend on me. We have a long journey to embark on together. Thank you for giving me the strength to fight it. Thank you my son. We will emerge VICTORIOUS!

13th June

Sameer was overjoyed. He now saw a wife determined to beat all the odds and overcome this dreaded condition. We hugged all night and promised to see each other through it.

I now felt the pain and trauma he had gone through. He knew of it much earlier than me. He had seen the reports of the first diagnostic center, but he couldn't let me know about it before a second confirmation. He pretended that the reports were lost just so that I wouldn't panic. What did he go through? *Dadi* and *dada* half dead with anxious concern but unable able to show it. I can't even begin to imagine Sameer's state of mind while I was retaking the tests. He must have been desperately praying for it to all be normal. What would he have felt when he tried to convince me about a blockage in the fallopian tubes which could hamper my second pregnancy ? He probably guessed that I would breakdown before the diagnosis was compete and kept pretending that nothing was wrong.

He was on the phone and net continually conferring with experts, sending reports around the world, consulting and co-coordinating while I thought he was losing it over some legal hassles related to some nameless property.

It is not impossible to vanquish cancer. Many have done it. I am young and strong and along with modern medical science, may have a good chance of beating the odds. We did a lot of research and finally decided to go to London for treatment. Now the question was about you, who would look after you? *Dadi-dada* felt very strongly that I should just leave you behind with them but I would not hear of it. There was no way that I could stay away from you. They tried along with *nani-nana* to convince me but to no avail. I had never been so adamant. Finally they gave in and it was decided that your *dadi* would come along with us. Sameer is booking an apartment and scheduling appointments with the doctors there. He has also applied for visas, for the four of us. Until then I am to undergo chemotherapy here under the guidance of Dr Shiv Shekar.

20th June

Chemotherapy is extremely painful son. I have been treated for 3 days and will have to go for another round soon. It is intravenously administered through a drip in the vein. I have never felt more ill than after the start of my chemotherapy. Vomiting, diarrhea, excessive fatigue, numbness in my limbs are all sapping me.

To make matters worse I've started shedding hair. It is scary seeing strands of hair everywhere; the pillow, bathtub, towel, and even at the dining table. Sameer is always with me now and has been instrumental in making the situation much more bearable. The visa call is scheduled for next week and your dad is leaving no stone unturned to see that our case is put on priority. The news of my having cancer seems to have spread like wildfire. The phone hardly stops ringing. Family, relatives, friends, acquaintances all offer their sympathies, but I do not speak to any of them. Their words pain me and at this stage I do not want anything to depress me or deter me from my goal. I am tired of answering their questions.

"Why did it have to be you?" Even I am yet to figure out the answer for that. Lot of visitors also drop in but Sameer sees to it that they are not around me for very long. I try to pray as often as I can. When I had much to thank God for, I never really remembered him or bothered acknowledging his gifts, but in my moment of crisis I have not forgotten to ask for his blessings every single day. My prayers are lengthy and frequent. They all end with me asking God to make me better again so that I can see my son grow up.

30th June

We got our visas sanctioned. We are leaving for London on the 7th of July. Sameer will be leaving a couple of days earlier to prepare everything for my arrival. Kajal *maasi* arrived today.

Dadi has probably told her about me being diagnosed with cancer, for whenever I see her, she always seemed teary eyed. I really wish we could take her along with us but the process to get a passport for her would take ages. I know it will be very difficult for *dadi* to manage looking after you there all by herself but she is happily doing it for my sake. *Nana*, *nani* too will be visiting us in London for a couple of weeks. I know that they are coming to help out with you. Siblings too will drop in. So it seems that we will have plenty of company there.

Dr Shiv Shekar has mentally prepared me for a major surgery which would probably be done within a few days of my arriving there. My uterus along with my fallopian tubes and both the ovaries will be removed. Along with it would go Sameer's dream of a large family. The notion saddens me everytime I think about it.

Our packing is being taken care of by *dadi*. What would I have done without her? I am all prepared to go to London armed with hopes, wishes, desires and expectations. Vatsal I don't want much; just to always be with you.

9th July

It is my 4th wedding anniversary today. And how am I spending it? By preparing for my surgery tomorrow. We had a small celebration in my hospital room. *Nani* and *nana* arrived yesterday night and joined in the cake cutting. Sameer gifted me a heart shaped gold pendent encrusted with rubies and diamonds. I bought him a small heart shaped locket which had a photo of mine in the left side. On the locket was inscribed.

Don't write my name on sand
Waves will wash it away
Don't write my name in sky
Wind may blow it away
Write my name in your heart
That's where it will forever stay

Tears ran down his cheeks and for the first time he broke down in front of me. We did not speak, just hugged each other and let our tears do all the talking. Nobody interrupted us. They walked away. This was just our moment. Today we expressed our feelings, fears, grievances, love and affection for each other through our tears. There were no barriers to stop them and they flowed freely. We did not want to let go of one another and hoped that by hugging each other tightly we would never have to say bye.

"I promise you Simi that on our next anniversary we will have a very grand celebration. It will be a very lavish one. All your friends, family, relatives will be there and we will........."

He kept talking without realizing what he was saying. All the while I just wanted to say. "Sameer all I want for my next anniversary is to just be there".

20th July

I survived the surgery son. In a lot of pain still. Had to stay in the hospital for 4 days and even now I am recuperating in the apartment. *Nani* and *dadi* are taking care of you. I requested them to keep you near me. Want to watch you all the time. Ravi and Simar will be here tomorrow. Ravi's romance has been put on hold for now. He insists that only after I totally recover will we go ahead with the engagement formalities.

You want me to hug you and hold you tight, but I am unable to fulfill these little wishes of yours. Can't wait to get well soon to change the situation.

Will have to go to the hospital for another round of tests, the doctors need to be sure that the cancer has not spread any further. I pray desperately that it has not. I don't want to deal with it anymore. I want my life back.

22nd July

It's been days since I last saw you laugh so much. Ravi and Simar have arrived and bought with them some much needed entertainment for you. They spend the day playing with you, and you finally have someone who can match your energy levels.

Spoke my heart out to Simar. Siblings are the best friends one can get. No matter what the situation is, they are always there for you. I am always going to regret my inability to give you this gift. Spoke about how difficult it was to come to terms with having my uterus removed. I shared my fears regarding the cancer having spread and about whether life would ever be the same again.

Got a pep talk on the art of positive thinking and its far reaching powers. Would need all of it for my tests tomorrow. Just hoping that everything is fine and I can finally head back to India.

Missing my country........my home........and my people.

28th July

The reports are not positive Vatsal. The cancer has spread to the liver and lungs. Doctors here are hoping to combat this with chemotherapy, but dread having to go through that torture again.

I am breaking down.

I can't handle it anymore.

God please stop this nightmare. How much more pain am I supposed to bear? How much more will my family have to go through?

The sad part of it is that they cannot guarantee a complete cure. The doctors are not able to tell me whether I will be cured after undergoing all their prescribed treatments. They are not even ready to guarantee me a few years of respite.

"You should have come earlier. Our chances would have been much better."

"Let's start the treatment and hope for the best."

"If we can destroy the cells then you may have a very long life ahead of you".

"But doctor what if the cells are not completely destroyed, then what..................then what is to happen to me?" This was always greeted by silence.

Sameer has been by my side through all this. He is trying his best to be brave and is pretending to be very positive, but I can see the fear and pain in his eyes too. I can see it on everyone's faces. *Dada* too is flying in today. My family is trying to cheer me up. But I don't want them to see me in so much of agony.

What if there is no hope for me? What is to then become of my parents? To see their child die a slow and painful death before their very eyes. What is to happen to Sameer? We vowed to always be together, but now I would be unable to fulfill those vows.

I was supposed to grow old with him. We used to talk about us in our eighties, sitting on a beach dressed in floral prints sharing a coconut. I used to tease Sameer about his hypothetical baldness and he would retort by answering that a fit old bald man would look better than a fat old woman. We would follow it up with a mock pillow fight which would end in uncontrollable peals of laughter. All this now seems like distant memories of things that would never be realized.

What is to happen to you Vatsal? You're my joy, my dream, the answer to all my prayers, my love and my world. A mother is everything to her child. You are supposed to see the world through my eyes. Even if I am away from you for a few hours you cry out plaintively- "*mummy chaahiye*". You need me. I have to recover, I have to see you grow, have to see you blossom into a fine young lad.

Yes son I will go through chemotherapy, will go through any surgery and any treatment to be fine. I will do anything to be with you baby.

5th August

I am going through a lot of pain, but your face my son gives me the strength to bear it. This round of chemotherapy is even more painful than the first one. Pain is lancing through me like hot coals. There are moments when I feel that I will be overwhelmed by this pain. My hands are becoming numb and it is getting more difficult for me to write to you.

10th August

Finished the third round of chemotherapy. The pain keeps increasing. Just want to throw up. Don't feel like eating anything. Feeling increasingly tired. Want to go back home.

Want us all to go back home.

5th September

Nana, *nani*, Ravi and Simar all left. I asked them to leave. Told them to get back to their normal lives. No point asking them to watch me suffer which pains them more. As they left I felt like I was bidding goodbye to my childhood. My adolescence flashed before my eyes. I saw myself coming home from school with my report card. I stood second in the class. I wasn't sure whether I should have been happy about being second or feel bad about losing out on the top position. It slowly faded away.

Another memory surfaced. I remembered my eighth birthday party where I refused to cut the cake because it was not the one I had previously selected. While everyone around was trying to coax me out of creating a scene in front of the guests, Ravi went ahead and cut my cake. A proper war then ensued.

I was in tears crying over my destroyed science project which Simar had accidentally spilled milk upon. While I bawled in one corner my siblings together compiled another project for me, which turned out better than the original. More often than not I would hide my library books in my school book covers and spend the evening leisurely reading them while mom thought that I was diligently studying. Those long hours of leching at hunks with Simar during college days while always looking out for Ravi hoping he was not around. Those seemingly endless holidays where my biggest fear was having all three of us share a room.

Endless hours spend in badgering our parents as to who was their favourite child and never being convinced about their reply of all being equally loved. Fights over whose choice of movie would be viewed, who would get to decide the day's meals, who would get to select a restaurant on Saturday nights and the biggest one; who started the fight. There was a time when I couldn't wait to grow up and today all I wish for is to go back to my childhood.

I want to head back home. The tests conducted after every chemotherapy session do not show any promise in the shrinkage of cancer cells. Rather it seems to have gotten worse in the liver.

Doctors are becoming less optimistic, Sameer is becoming more miserable. He is moving around in a very dejected manner. He prays wherever he can, but God is probably in no mood to listen to him. I am beginning to lose hope too, finding it more difficult to deal with the increasing pain. Hate to look into the mirror. A gaunt, tired old lady stares back at me. Why am I going through all this? I ask myself this question often; but after seeing your face I understand. I am going through all the pain just for one tiny hope that I cling to. The hope that I can see my son's childhood. The hope that I can accompany you on your first day to school. That I can participate in all the joys of you growing up. Be able to attend your parent teacher meetings. See you have your first crush and be able to console you with your heartbreaks. To plan play dates for you, plan your parties every year and be amazed at your changing career choices.

How can I stop fighting for life when there is still so much to live for? I can't say bye to you. God please let me live, I do not want to die, please give me enough time to raise my son.

10th September

We are going back to India. I want to now go back to my country, my city and be amidst my people. Didn't take too much to convince Sameer about it. The treatment isn't helping me. My condition has not improved and the doctors are not hopeful about my chances. It is a very dull and empty life here not just for me but for *dadi*, Sameer and you as well. I miss my friends, relatives and home.

Relatives previously seemed so irritating as they often came in unannounced, stayed longer than required and tended to make my life tough, but today I yearn for them to come and talk to me. London is beautiful but not from the perspective of someone confined to a hospital room.

Miss my country and my city. I will continue with the treatment in Bangalore itself. The chances are as good there as here so I might as well head back. My birthday is coming up and I want to be able to cut my cake in my house. Home is where I belong.

Where we belong.

15th September

Back home, Sameer fulfilled his promise of getting me to cut my cake at home. Pushpa *bhua* had done up the whole house, called my friends, parents, relatives. She's been managing the house in *dadi*'s absence. She had been performing pujas for me almost every day. Papa informs me that she has been to every *temple, church* and *gurdwara* to pray for my long life. It is in such situations that the real nature of people surfaces. How I used to hate having her over and now I can't thank her enough.

I asked Sameer not to get me any gifts this year. I instead wanted a promise from him. I asked him to promise me that he would always be happy and keep you happy. Whatever the situation in life, there should never be any tears of sadness in your eyes. He tried to avoid it by saying that it was up to me to keep you both happy.

I know son it is my duty to ensure the happiness of my family but I get the feeling that I will not be able to fulfill my duties for much longer.

16th September

Met Dr Shiv Shekar yesterday and the results of the tests showed that the cancer had spread and was now in the fourth stage. The doctor asked me to wait outside the room and spoke to Sameer privately. They had a lengthy discussion. When Sameer came out of the room, he did not tell me anything, but his face was grim. He had the appearance of an absolutely defeated man. I guess now it is just a matter of time for me. But how much was the question.

20th September

In life, death is the only certainty but we still try to run from it. Since I have taken birth I have to die, why do I then want to deny it? Life has given me a lot; a wonderful childhood, loving parents, caring siblings, a dream partner in Sameer, indulgent in laws and an angel like you. I had been blessed with fortune and happiness. My life has been nothing short of the sort of fairytale most people would only dream about. Many have told me that I was amongst the lucky few chosen by God, but I should have known that even fairytales have to come to an end. I did not have any qualms while accepting life's presents. I never questioned why I had been showered with so much largesse, when there was a dearth of it everywhere.

Why then do I not want to accept this lifespan that I have been deemed fit for? Why I am gullible enough to believe everybody's personal solution for my condition? Someone tells about a *ved* in their village who can cure terminal diseases. Another person talks to me of a homeopath who can perform miracles. Yet another speaks of a temple where all wishes are granted. Somebody else gave me a black thread from a sacred and holy *dargah*. I am ready to try it all.

I am lost in an endless ocean of hopelessness and I am desperate enough to cling to any hope. Life had given me everything, how could I now let death take it all away from me?

30th September

Chemotherapy is of no help now. The cancer is now rapidly spreading and the doctors kindly let us know this. What would I now like to do? Keep trying chemotherapy or radiation or would I like to take pain killers to ease the pain which was gradually increasing? This is the end of my fight. All the modern advances of science are to no avail.

Man is sending satellites into deep space, inventing deadlier weapons by the day, creating gizmos which are beyond imagination but we are still unable to find cure for a disease which has been humanity's scourge for many ages. Every day I read about people succumbing to cancer but they were always names of faceless people. I would turn over to the next page without giving it a second thought. People died of cancer all the time, so what?

I feel differently now that I am about to be a part of that statistic. What difference will another name make to the never ending list?

It will make a difference to me. It will make a difference to all the promises I have made to my family and myself, which I will now be unable to fulfill. What about all my dreams which I am yet to realize? It will affect the vows I had made to Sameer at the time of marriage. Going around the sacred fire I had promised to be his partner for life. To see him through sickness and health. My death will affect a future which we had imagined as experiencing together.

How many years do I have? The doctor does not reply. It then struck me that I probably do not have that kind of time. Here I am thinking about years when I probably just have a few months ahead of me. "With the help of medicines we can assume that you have 4-8 months."

4-8 months is the time, life has granted me. Is this all that God has bestowed me with despite all the prayers on my behalf? Why is nobody's prayer being answered? How can I do it all in just a few months? How am I supposed to see the world? How am I supposed to watch you turn into a handsome young man or share a coconut on a beach with my aging husband? Vatsal how do I do it all?

You aren't going to be more than 2 ½ years when the time comes. How can God snatch the mother of one so young? What is to become of you? What is to become of us? Will you have any memories of me? Will you even be able to recollect me? Fear grips me and refuses to let go. What happens to one after death?

When I was young I had read stories about the soul being sent to heaven or hell depending on one's deeds. Where would I be going? Some stories spoke about rebirth; would I experience one? What would I be reborn as? It doesn't matter though. My entity as Simran would end forever.

I want peace.

I want to come to terms with my situation. God please give me strength to face this judgment you've pronounced on me. If you have inflicted the wound then you must also provide me with the firmness to reconcile with it. I need it now more than ever.

5th October

Today I have reached a decision. I now accept my destiny. What time is left will now be utilized to its fullest. I want to live my life (whatever is left of it) to the best of my abilities. Want to share every moment of it with my loved ones. Want to complete many things left undone, talk with and meet people whom I hadn't met for years, see places that have I've always desired to visit and most importantly complete my diary. Sameer has asked me to relax instead of writing, but how can I stop this means of communication with you? This diary along with photographs and videos will be all that will remain of your mother.

It will be my lasting legacy for you. Words which I would have spoken to you over the years will now have to be expressed through this diary. It will be our special link. When you feel the need for a mother (which you often will) and don't see me around, then read this. You will understand my love, my care, my feelings and emotions for you. This is not literature, but a conversation; a collection of my feelings, emotions and experiences, a saga of the highs and lows which I have faced in the roller coaster called Life ever since you entered it.

A bouquet of joyous moments when I have laughed so hard that tears have rolled down. A bucket of tears that I have shed till there were no more to spare.

I am trying to figure out how to live a lifetime in a span of a few moments. Yet my dear son I try to be thankful for each passing day as it gives me that much more time to spend with you.

I want you to always be in front of me. I want to start every morning I have left, with you by my side. When I lie down on my pillow to sleep I want you to be next to me. Son I want to give you as much love as possible and take as many memories with me as I can.

7th October

I have made a bucket-list of the things I want to do. Want to share them with you.

1. Write to you
2. Convince *nani* and *nana* to go ahead with Ravi's engagement and wedding so I can be a part of it.
3. Meet my friends and speak to all of them wherever they maybe.
4. Spend time with my extended family from both the sides.
5. Travel to holiday destinations I've always wanted to visit.
6. Make a video of us and our special moments.
7. Open an orphanage. Had always wanted to do it. Had it in mind for later, but now, obviously before time runs out.
8. No more chemotherapy and radiation, just pain killers which will help me carry on while I can.
9. To share a coconut with Sameer while I watch you play on pristine beach.

Showed my to-do list to Sameer. He got angry and told me not to give up. "We will try in America," he said. "You can't quit now. Please think about me and Vatsal. You cannot give up for our sake, you cannot. Willpower can overcome the greatest of hurdles. Every day, even as we speak, new treatments are being invented. Something might soon be discovered. You've got to hang in there. I will see you through. Together we will come across a cure." He pleaded with a quivering voice. He was trembling!

"Sameer please do not live in denial. We all know that there is no further hope. Why do you want me to spend the remaining days in a hospital in vain? If there was even a ray of hope I would cling on to it. I would have continued to fight tooth and nail even if it was but the slimmest possible chance, but you know there isn't any. I do not want to fool myself. Please help me enjoy whatever is left. I can't take any more chemotherapy. Please don't put me through more pain. Let my last days be full of love and happiness. I want to be in my home with my family around me, not on some hospital bed surrounded by doctors and nurses. I love you Sameer and want to hear you say you love me too. I don't want to die before I have to. If you love me then please let me live the way I want to, while I still can." I broke down on in his arms.

Sameer struck number 8 on my list off.

8th October

Today's was spent in trying to convince Ravi to go ahead with his engagement to Anushka. It was a very difficult task. *Nana* and *nani* refused at first. "Beta you get well and then we will think of the marriage." They were still in denial. Sameer used all his convincing powers and after lots of persuasion, they were ready. Ravi though was totally different matter altogether. He refused to budge. "Not till my Simi is fine." We all tried to persuade him but he did not relent. Finally I asked him, "Would you rather have me welcome my bhabhi home in person or as a garlanded photo on the wall when she walks in."

Ravi finally agreed.

10th October

Today Kajal *maasi*'s passport arrived. Sameer had applied for it in July and it's now finally here. We want to travel to foreign destinations along with you. I am now unable to run behind you. Sorry son but my body can no longer exert itself. Now that she can travel, so can we. I refused to leave you behind. How can I afford to spend a moment away from you let alone a day? After all, there are not too many of those left.

Sameer has applied for visas to Australia and New Zealand. Had been wanting to visit New Zealand from the time I watched *The lord of the rings*.

The wedding date for Ravi is yet to be finalized but it is tentatively being scheduled either for 10th December or 16th January. Nobody is complaining about the short notice because they all know and understand the situation.

We played a lot with you. Sameer shot videos of us playing *peek a boo*, me singing rhymes to you, stacking blocks and me pushing you in your tricycle. Will have to talk Sameer into getting back to work. It has been months since he actually spent a whole day at work. Papa is looking after everything but the increased workload is now starting to affect him.

12th October

The pain is again starting to increase. Will be going to Dr Shiv Shekar to relieve it. All of us went out for breakfast today. *Dada* and *dadi* reserved the entire restaurant for us. I was so surprised to see the whole restaurant empty. Generally, we have to wait for quite some time for a table. "Why did you do this papa"? I asked surprised.

"Do you remember once when we were all watching an episode of *Family comes first,* the actor books the entire restaurant for his fiancée's birthday and you exclaimed 'Oh I wish somebody would do it for me too? Have wanted to do this for you from a very long time."

I smiled but my heart ached. It wanted to cry out, papa don't make it more difficult for me to say goodbye.

15th October

Sameer refuses to listen to me. He is not ready to even talk about it. "Simi I have agreed to everything you said and asked of me. You refused to go for chemotherapy; you do not want to go to America for treatment. You talk about doing this and that before you are no longer there with us........" his voice was loud and lips were quivering, "and now you are asking me to leave you and go to work? Simi, have you ever spared a thought about me or my feelings. Do you even have an idea of the pain I am going through? What is supposed to happen to me seeing you in this state? How despondent am I at the thought of losing you? I can't even begin to come to terms with it. You don't want to stay away from Vatsal even for a few hours and yet think that that I would be able to stay apart from you? How will I be able to concentrate on work?

It is just work and I will manage it, but please don't ever ask me not to be by your side."

I never raised this issue again.

20th October

Our visas have arrived! We will be travelling to Australia and New-Zealand! I wanted to celebrate your 2nd birthday in Australia. This reminds me, Ravi's wedding date has been finalized for 10th December. It will be held in Bangalore as travelling, will by then become very difficult. I wish to celebrate while I still can. Want to enjoy and make the most of every occasion that comes my way.

Now only if I could do something to my appearance to make it match my spirits. I actually look like a scary version of my previous self. All the chemotherapy and medicines have caused too much weight and hair loss and have left me looking drained and pale. I don't go in front of the mirror much. Why let it remind me of my destiny which I've accepted for myself? In fact I could challenge all the make-up artists and the best hair dressers to make me look like my former self and every one of them would lose.

But Sameer says that I have always looked beautiful to him and will continue to do so. If only everybody could see me through his eyes.

I have caught up with quite a few of my friends recently and keep making plans of meeting them. They are all aware of my predicament but thankfully do not vocally sympathize. Rather they remind me of shared childhood memories and make me smile. Feels good to walk down the memory lane. When I hear what they've achieved, I initially feel a little bad, but then I realize later that I too have achieved a lot. I have helped create a family with love, trust, care and concern. A family which has given me everything I could have asked for and a lot more. A family which is standing by me in my hour of need. I've finally become the daughter my in laws have always yearned for. My husband has found a companion and soul mate. I've given birth to a son who is the apple of everyone's eyes. This is no mean feat and today I am far more proud of my accomplishments then otherwise. Being a homemaker is one of the toughest jobs and I take pride in saying that I have performed this role very well.

You love to talk and I love to listen. You go on and on about the stories I tell you, though you get it all mixed up. Together we watch your favorite channel, *Animal Planet*. Many times I have had to change it before you happen to see a lion attack a baby deer, because if you did, then it would probably have you in crying for hours. We look at snaps together. You clap in glee at every photo and tell me whose it is.

Have sorted them out and even dated them. Sat and compiled and updated all our photo albums. What better memories than photographs?

1st November

HAPPY BIRTHDAY VATSAL!

Many happy returns of the day my love, my pride and my joy. May you live a hundred years and may you be blessed with all the happiness in the world. We are in Australia. You have turned two today and you celebrated it in Aussie style. The journey was very tiring despite the business class seats. Kajal *maasi* was in awe of the flight and exclaimed loudly in joy upon seeing the flat bed seats which embarrassed Sameer. We are in Sydney. We made you cut the cake below the Harbor Bridge. Then we headed to the Opera house. A quick tour and then back to our hotel. Cannot move much and tire very easily. You were excited initially but soon became weary and just wanted to be carried around. This responsibility was equally shared between Sameer and Kajal *maasi.*

We had a lot of calls from family. *Dadi* missed you a lot and assured you of a big party once you were back.

3rd November

Today we went to the 12 apostles. We are now in Melbourne staying next to the Great Ocean Road. Traveled by helicopter. Had to leave you behind for a couple of hours with Kajal *maasi.* It was indeed a breathtaking sight. We are here for another night and then we head for the gold coast. I know we are moving too fast. You hardly get to settle down and then we are already off to the next destination, but baby we are pressed for time.

8th November

Explored Gold Coast, Cairns and Brisbane. Especially enjoyed the Great Barrier Reef. A large part of the trip was done on a wheelchair. Body now does not permit too much of walking. A quick trip to New-Zealand before we head back. Food is becoming a major issue for both of us. You are very picky and I can't digest most things.

14th November

Happy Children's Day. You celebrated your birthday in Australia and Children's day in New –Zealand. The scenic beauty here is breathtaking. Snow-capped mountains, innumerable waterfalls along the way to Milford Sound, lush green trees and clear lakes are a traveler's delight. I did a very quick heli tour of the glacier in Franz Joseph.

We went to both the North and South islands and visited the cities of Auckland, Queenstown, Rotoura and Wellington. I had never seen such a beautiful combination of greenery and snow. The weather was chilly, despite it being the summer here. We were well insulated though and when you go through the snaps you might mistake yourself for an Eskimo. The exotic fruits available here are to die for, especially the cherries.

Well it has been a fantastic trip, though the travelling did take its toll on all of us. We are now heading back for India tonight via Singapore. Can't wait to have home cooked food again.

25th November

My apologies for writing after such a long gap. A lot took place in the last 10 days and just did not get the time to write. Will fill in the details. After returning from New-Zealand the pain in the abdomen became unbearable and I had to be hospitalized for a couple of days. To be honest I panicked as I wondered whether my grant on time was up. The doctors bought it under control but the dose of pain killers are now of a higher potency. Everybody was in a state of absolute fright and did not leave my room until the doctor assured them that there was no danger to my life (as of now). You fell ill and were down with a viral fever. It was indeed a very testing time. You wanted me and only me to attend to your needs. Both the doctors and my health did not permit it. I cursed myself a lot for being so weak. While you howled for me, I cried for you. Sameer was torn between pacifying you and me, but those days are now behind us. By God's grace you are now healthy again.

We were in talks to adopt an orphanage near our house. We have already started funding it to cover its expenditure, while trying to have it named after me. What's in a name you might ask, but for me it's all about leaving behind a memorable mark of my passage. I am as apprehensive about being forgotten as I am about dying.

The lawyers are working on it round the clock, but since plenty of legal groundwork is involved, it will take a lot of time. The question now is if I have that kind of time.

30th November

Family and some close relatives have started arriving. Preparations for the wedding have begun. Practice for the *sangeet* has commenced. I won't be participating, but can at least look forward to everyone's company. It was so much fun during Simar's wedding. The amount we had laughed, especially watching Sameer dance. He is ready to dance to any number, provided I laugh as much as the last time. I guess this is the last time I will be meeting most of my relatives.

It is so surreal, the way I use the word *last.* As each month passes by, I tell myself that this is the last of my life. Any trip is probably the last to a given location. I keep thinking that this is going to be the last chance I get to do something.

Before I go to sleep I pray for it to not be my last night. I have got to try to be thankful for each day rather than cry over the fact that there weren't too many left ahead of me.

Anushka is a lovely girl. Her beautiful face is matched by a very sweet disposition. She appears taller than her 5 feet 4 inches because of her slender figure. Doe like brown eyes, a sharp nose and high cheekbones are all wonderful but her standout feature, was her hazel coloured waist length thick wavy hair which left me in awe (also left me feeling wistful about my now long gone hair). We spent time with each other and spoke about my cancer.

There was no doubt, that they made a lovely pair and I liked her from the word go and the best part is that she loves you, my baby.

5th December

The engagement ceremony went off without a hitch despite the short notice. The only shortcoming (if can be called that) was that some of my parent's cousins could not make it, but I guess better them than me. Simar and Aakash joined us this morning. Aakash has put on quite a bit of weight; in fact he now sports a pot belly. Spent the day listening to Simar talk endlessly about her new family, her beautiful marriage and irritating neighbors.

It was difficult for me to mingle with the other guests while trying to ignore their sympathetic glances and mutedly shocked expressions. Ravi had assured me that no one would express pity or concern or bring up the subject, including *nana* and *nani.* I could definitely stay away from it all. Nothing was said to me directly, but they more than made up for it behind my back.

Fortunately there were other experiences to make up for this. Gaurav hardly left me alone. He is one person whom I can speak candidly with and know that all I said would remain safe with him. He showed me the box where he had kept all my *rakhis* over the years. He was an only child and he always looked up to me as a sister and not cousin. We had once fought stupidly over some silly game. I got angry and told him that he didn't care about me. He replied, "I care more for you than what you do for me. You have another brother in Ravi but I don't have a little sister". I looked sadly at the *rakhis*, fully aware that there would be no further additions to the box ever.

8th December

Watched all the ceremonies without participating in most of them. The pain is rapidly increasing and the medicines aren't helping much. Losing control over my limbs too. I am unable to write for long. I keep lying down on the sofa in the hall so I can at least see what's going on.

Vatsal, I can feel the end drawing near and I am feeling scared. As each day passes my fear increases. I want to hold on to you and hide somewhere. A place where death won't be able to find me. I can see it on everybody's faces. They laugh and smile in front of me but away from me, I know that they cry. Sometimes I think it would have been better if I had died in an accident. Then I would not have to anticipate the gradual approach of death every single day and see the pained anguish of my loved ones.

I feel thankful however that I got the chance to at least say bye. To tell everyone what they meant to me. To hear how they felt about me. We take life for granted. We forget to say words that we so badly want to say, because we think that these feelings can wait. Wrong! Son, *live everyday to the fullest.* Live in the moment. Love like there is no tomorrow. Don't plan for retirement when you are yet to savor youth. Don't put anything off for later, for you may never know when you have to call it quits. Don't ever take relationships for granted or expect second chances. They just might never come your way again. Never wait for the right time to express your feelings. There is no better time than now.

15th December

The guests have all left after the wedding yesterday. Today, I fainted. I was rushed to Dr.Shiv Shekhar's hospital. Tests show that the cancer has reached a terminal phase, faster than expected. Fresh medicines were prescribed yet again. I had to stay there for 3 days and was actually asked to get myself admitted in the hospital. I suppose it means that it was going to be over soon, but I did not want to stay in the hospital. I wanted to go home and cried till Sameer was convinced that home was the best option. My room now resembles a hospital room. It has an oxygen cylinder, a very large tray filled with many medicines and a monitor to check my pulse along with a nurse to look after me round the clock.

20th December

The medicines have helped. Feel a little more energetic now. I am able to walk up to the hall and kitchen where I can sit and play with you for a little while. I want to do so much more. Like completing my bucket list. I told Sameer about my beachside fantasy with him. The very next day while I slept in the guest room, he set to work in my room. When I entered, I was stunned to see a large screen which displayed a seaside vista. The entire floor was covered with sand. Vatsal, you were squealing in delight and playing with your sand kit. There were shells scattered all over. Sameer was invitingly holding a coconut with two straws. I was at a loss of words not knowing whether to laugh or cry; did both.

25th December

Today I became Santa. Visited *Sharada Ashram* (or *Simran Hridalaya* as it will shortly be known). My name on a large sign was all but ready to be displayed. Just a few more weeks of legal formalities to go through. I was in a wheel chair being pushed by Sameer with you in my lap. It was a small orphanage which housed around 50 children, but looked very different from the time I last visited it. The walls had been painted. Each room had a different color and pattern on its walls. All the rooms had beds with pillows and blankets. There were cupboards with each child being given a shelf. The bathroom had been redone with new plumbing and quality fittings. The dining room had two long tables with chairs for everyone. It was lunchtime and I felt good seeing the children eat a healthy meal where second helpings weren't refused.

The caretaker was a kind, middle aged woman who briefed us about the developments taking place. She also introduced us to the four teachers who would be teaching, English, Kannada, Math and Science to the children. It was now time for gifts. We distributed school bags with age appropriate books, stationery and lunch boxes. It was so heartwarming to see the joy on the faces of all the children. The largesse didn't end there though, as Sameer then bought two large cartons. These contained gift wrapped boxes of various shapes and sizes. This was a pleasant surprise even for me. Turns out that your dad had asked each kid about the one gift which he would like to receive more than anything else. He then compiled their wish list and arranged for those things to be picked up. The name of each child has been written upon each box. He made me distribute all of these gifts. The presents were then unwrapped. Some had asked for watches, some clothes, a few wanted sneakers and others, bats. They came to hug me. Many had tears of gratitude in their eyes. God is really funny when it came to determining destinies. These children were so thankful for the trivial little things they received while you as a single child had so much luxury bestowed upon him. Then again, who are we to question his decisions? After giving you all the luxury and love, was he now not taking your mother away from you?

I wanted to thank Sameer for this beautiful moment, but he instead thanked me.

"Thank you so much Simi for bringing so many children in my life. I had always wanted three but thanks to you I now have 50. I promise you that these children will be provided with the best facilities and opportunities. They will want for nothing. Every night before sleeping when they say their prayers, they will remember you."

1st January 2006

HAPPY NEW YEAR Vatsal! May you always be very happy and healthy. I now start my mornings and end my day by saying "I love you" to Sameer and you. Every night before sleeping, I ask God to grant me one more morning with you. Each day now seems like a gift which can be snatched away anytime. *Nana* and *nani* want to be with me now. They will be flying in tomorrow. Ravi wanted to join them but I dissuaded him. "There is still time Ravi."

I have to be helped around in a wheel chair. Food now consists simply of thin porridges of different kinds. Pain killers seem to have stopped working and there are days when it becomes unbearable, but I still want to cling to life's fragile thread. I promise you that I will not let go until it's no longer possible to hold on. I want to be able to hug you, to feel you, to hear your heartbeat, to watch you smile, to see you dance and to be a part of it as long as I possibly can.

Yesterday night *dada* and I spoke for quite some time.

"Simi *beta* I want to say sorry for not being able to help you"

"Papa why do you say so? You have done everything possible, but you have to understand that we are not capable of defying God's will."

"How can I imagine life without my daughter? What would I not do to take your place?"

"Till I came in this house you had not known the love of a daughter. You will return to the same state once I depart. Also, am I not leaving behind lots of memories? Papa, please do not weaken my resolve. You have each other to turn to, while I leave empty handed, though I hope to take your love and blessings with me. You have showered me with a lifetime of affection in just a few years, for that I am extremely grateful. I want to confess to something- you are dearer to me than mummy, but promise me that you will never tell her this."

Could not complete the conversation as he left the room in tears.

16th January

Vatsal my child I now can see my time slipping away. I am not sure when, but know for certain that it won't be long now. I have now made my peace with my destiny. I had gone through shock, denial, anger, frustration, tears, fear and now I have finally come to terms with my fate. A little while ago, I kept saying 'if only I did not have cancer', 'if only I had got myself tested earlier', 'if only I had more moments to cherish'. I kept hoping that I might wake up in the morning just to realize that it had all been a bad dream. That I could be miraculously cured. But life, my son life is not about ifs and buts. Life is what it is and not what it should be. Yesterday I watched the movie *Anand* which starred *Rajesh Khanna.* He portrayed a young man who did not have very long to live, but instead of being gloomy about the situation, he lived it in such a manner so as to bring joy to all those around. His character showed me that death could only end your life but couldn't and shouldn't be allowed to snatch the joy of living. Death does not concern us, because as long as we exist, death is not here. And when it is, we no longer exist. Today I hold no grudges, no longer question God and don't blame medical science for being impotent. I am thankful that I am with my family. All my loved and dear ones are around me. I got a chance to fulfill my dreams, to sort out things, to be able to say bye to everyone. How many are lucky enough to do that? There are so many who die unexpectedly everyday. They don't even get a chance to say goodbye. I was at least fortunate enough to get that opportunity. I had a wonderful life with a great childhood, wedded bliss and beautiful motherhood. Today there are no complaints. I will not deny that I am a little scared in facing death; I don't know what it will be like.

But I do know that I am thankful to life for showering its blessings upon me in the form of my parents, my siblings, Sameer, my in-laws and best of all, YOU. May you see all your dreams come true and achieve outstanding things. May you be blessed with health, happiness and love to your heart's content. Live every moment deeply. Love like there is no tomorrow. Cherish every small moment of happiness that comes your way. Be true to all your relations.

Remember, not everyday will be a sunny day. There will also be dark, rainy and gloomy days. Be patient for the sun is never far away. Even in the midst of disappointment never lose hope. Learn from yesterday, live for today and hope for tomorrow. As *William W.Purkey said-* you've *got to dance like there's nobody watching. Love like you'll never be hurt. Sing like you mean it and live like it's heaven on earth*"

Son, I was previously afraid that once I was gone, I might not be a part of the memory of my loved ones, specifically, you. Children when it comes to remembering their mothers are able to recollect many instances. How she would reprimand them for their mistakes, praise them for their achievements, encourage them when they felt defeated and be by their side always, offering unconditional support. But I am afraid that you my son will have no such recollections. Maybe this diary, a small attempt on my part, will remind you about me. I have asked Sameer to give it to you when he feels that you will be old enough to emotionally understand it. It will take you through a time of which you'll have no recollections, not even ones which are faint.

This diary will give you a glimpse of me. It will help you understand your mother. It will rollback the years to a time when you and I lived in one another's love. When all that mattered to you was me. It will show you that I was no different from every other mother. I am aware that there will be many instances in your life when you will miss me. What would I not give to be a part of your life? But I am helpless. I want you to know that your mother was very brave when her end came. This diary is for you. It is to be our special way of telling each other how much we cared about one another. When you grow up and your dad tells you stories of when you were an infant; tell him that you already know about it.

I am so glad that I had maintained this diary for us. When I started I had wanted it to be a reminder of all our beautiful moments; little did I know that it would be our only surviving bond to withstand the test of time. I may no longer physically exist in your world but there is no stopping me from living on in your memories. Son, you have always been my world and this is a small attempt from me to continue to be a part of yours.

17th January

In a short while now I will have to say good bye,
Away from your reach I will go up high.
In leaving you I feel sorrow and pain,
The emotions inside I could never explain.
Please cherish those memories we shared,
Remember me as a person that genuinely cared.
Promise me that when I rest in peace,
My memories and image you must never release.
For death leaves a heartache no one can heal,
But Love leaves behind a memory no one can steal.

28th January

Vatsal this is your father writing. Simi is no longer with us. On the 20th, her beautiful soul left us forever. There was complete tranquility on her face. In her last moments, she was surrounded by all her loved ones and she spoke to each one of us privately. There were prayer sessions in her room through the day and into the night. She wanted it. She spoke about how we both made her life beautiful, about how we gave meaning to her existence. How, in a short span of time, we had given her immeasurable joy. She was leaving us physically but she would continue to live forever in our memories.

But son I wanted to be with her in person. I wanted to be able to hold her, to talk to her and to tell how much I love her. I knew this day would come eventually, but when it finally did, I wasn't prepared for it. We were supposed to spend our life together, but she's gone forever after just a few years. How can this void within me be filled? She wanted me to move on in life. Find love again.

But love can only happen once. No one can ever take her

place. Whose laughter will replace hers? Who will be able to talk to me endlessly? Whose eyes can have the affection she had for you? Who can be as concerned about our slightest of pain as her? Vatsal, no one can ever be a part of our lives like her. She asked me to be brave and take care of everyone else. Today somebody's lost a daughter, a sister, a daughter-in-law, a friend, but our loss is if anything, much greater. We have lost everything. She wasn't just a part of our world; she was our world in its entirety. How do I console others when I myself am so broken within? What would I have not done to be in her place? How many times had I prayed to let it be me instead of her? People keep telling me that God needs good people by his side and that this was her destiny, but does He not realize that we needed her too? She said that she is leaving us in each other's care.

"I want both my loves to be there for one another always. Sameer you will give our son the love of both a mother and father. Promise me that he will never have tears in his eyes and be in a situation where he would miss his mother. It will not be easy raising him up on your own, but Sameer I know you will do it and you will do it amazingly well. When our Vatsal grows up, I want him to say the love you showered him with more than made up for the loss of his mother. Promise me that".

I hope son that I can live up to my promise. She taught me what love was all about. A couple of weeks ago she asked me what I loved the most about her. I said everything. I loved her character, her quirks, her sense of humour, her smile, her smell, her touch, her pranks, her laughter; everything. She loved you and me wholeheartedly and unconditionally. She taught me that true love is enough to last us a lifetime. Her memories are one thing that death cannot take away from us. It will forever remain safe with us. I promise you son that they will never fade with the passage of time. She will forever continue to live in them.

Daddy

Acknowledgements

Thank you Manish for making this book possible. I do not have enough words to express my gratitude for you and acknowledge everything you have done. This book is as much your dream as mine. There are a few many more who have contributed immensely to my book and I would like to take this opportunity to thank them.

My children Aman and Sahil who provided me with enough experiences to help conceptualize the book and are now very excited about seeing the book in their school library.

My father in law, mother in law, dad and mom for all your encouragement, love and support. Hope to have done you proud today.

Savita, my sister who patiently sat through my narration every afternoon forgoing her sleep. Your appreciative and critical comments inspired me to carry on with my story.

Adi, Harshi, Viji, Reshu and my family members for your helpful inputs.

My uncle Surendra Choraria, who has been instrumental in the publication and launch of the book, thank you for your blessings and guidance.

My editor Prithvi, thank you for assisting me with sanitizing the content of this book.

I am also grateful to my publishers for being wonderfully understanding and supportive.

Lastly but by no means the least, my readers, thank you for selecting my book and thus making the entire experience worthwhile.

□□□